QUEENS AND MONSTERS

ALEATHA ROMIG

NEW YORK TIMES BESTSELLING AUTHOR

Book #4 of the Brutal Vows series

Aleatha Romig's Most Recent and Upcoming Releases

Visit Aleatha's store to purchase e-books, signed books, and store exclusive items. Link available on her website: aleatharomig.com

TO HAVE AND TO HOLD - Brutal Vows, book five - March 2025

Arranged marriage, Mafia/cartel, enemies to lovers, age-gap, he falls first, protective hero, Romeo and Juliet vibes, dangerous romance

QUEENS AND MONSTERS - Brutal Vows, book four - January 2025

Arranged marriage, Mafia/cartel, alpha hero, virgin heroine, touch her and die, family saga, he falls first, possessive hero, sheltered heroine, dangerous romance

BOUND BY A PROMISE – Brutal Vows, book three - October 2024

Arranged marriage, age-gap, forbidden, Mafia/cartel dangerous stand-alone romance

ONE STRING – July 2024

Aleatha's Lighter Ones - Second-chance, enemies-to-lovers, fake-date, little-sister's-best-friend, forbidden, stand-alone contemporary romance

TILL DEATH DO US PART- Brutal Vows, book two - June 2024

Arranged marriage, enemies to lovers, Mafia/cartel, he falls first, stand-alone, dangerous romance

NOW AND FOREVER – Brutal Vows, book one - May 2024

Arranged marriage, age-gap, Mafia/cartel stand-alone romance

LIGHT DARK – April 2024

Cult, psychological thriller, forced proximity, romantic suspense stand-alone

*Previously published through Thomas and Mercer as INTO THE LIGHT and AWAY FROM THE DARK

REMEMBERING PASSION – Sinclair Duet book one – September 2023

Scorching hot, second-chance romance filled with the suspense and intrigue

REKINDLING DESIRE – Sinclair Duet, book two – October 2023

Scorching hot, second-chance romance filled with the suspense and intrigue

SYNOPSIS~

Mafia/cartel, arranged marriage, forbidden, possessive hero, sheltered heroine, he falls first, dangerous romance

Reinaldo Rodríguez

Emiliano Ruiz

Both are dangerous, deadly, and powerful. Both are second-generation soldiers proving themselves in the Roríguez cartel.

Both want me. Of course, I wasn't told until it was too late. That's the way things work in the famiglia. My fate is up to Dario Luciano, my guardian.

He doesn't care about the way the men make me feel. How when I'm near them, the air crackles and my skin warms with stinging electricity, stirring something deep inside me that never before existed.

One fills me with desire, twisting my insides.

The other recognizes my need to be loved, filling me with a comfortable warmth.

By the time I learn that both have requested my hand, a deal has been brokered.

Neither man from the Roríguez cartel will have me.

I've been promised to another, the son of Dario's sworn enemy.

Will I have any say in my future?

What will happen to the alliance between the Luciano famiglia and the Roríguez cartel when tragedy strikes?

Have you been Aleatha'd?

QUEENS AND MONSTERS is a stand-alone dangerous Mafia/cartel romance in the "Brutal Vows" series. Each arranged-marriage story is filled with the suspense, intrigue, and heat you've come to expect from New York Times bestselling author Aleatha Romig.

PROLOGUE~

Dario Luciano
Capo dei capi, Kansas City

Leaning forward, I stared across my desk and around my office, taking in the famiglia's colleagues. Dante, my consigliere and also my brother, stood by my side. While the famiglia and the cartel had come to trust one another, that didn't mean we weren't cautious. Dante was armed to the teeth and so was I. Undoubtedly, we weren't the only ones. Our guests were equally prepared. The knives and guns in this office would set magnetometers off in a symphony of alarms.

While the ladies were out in the apartment preparing our holiday meal—the official reason for the cartel's visit—there was urgent business that needed to be discussed.

"Your father?" I asked Aléjandro.

The second-in-command of the Roríguez cartel was married to my sister, Mia. He nodded as his dark stare briefly met his brother Reinaldo's. "*Our padre,*" Aléjandro replied, sitting straighter, "is on his way." He looked down at his gold watch and back at me. "There was a change of plans to help with security."

Out of the corner of my eye, I watched Andrés Ruiz, father of both my wife, Catalina, and Dante's wife, Camila. With his arms crossed over his chest, the seams of his suit coat strained and his paunch hung over his belt. Visually, it was obvious that Andrés wasn't in the same fighting condition as the rest of us. Yet his age and experience sought respect. Without saying a word, his disapproval regarding the Roríguez cartel's newly declared hierarchy was evident in his narrowed eyes and the straight line of his pressed-together lips. His attention went to Aléjandro, the drug lord's eldest son. "Change of plans? Our plane was waiting for him in San Diego." His arms fell to his side. "I wasn't informed of a change."

My uncles Carmine and Salvatore were standing against the opposite wall, intently watching the exchange.

Clenching my teeth, the muscles in the side of my face tightened as trepidation squeezed my chest. "We are all working together, Andrés. That's why you're being informed."

Andrés nodded, resuming his position leaning against the bookcase. It was difficult for a man like him to take orders from younger men and it showed. Nevertheless, I was capo dei capi of Kansas City and my word was law. Jorge, the drug lord of the cartel, made the decision to place Aléjandro as his second-in-command.

Andrés could choose to disagree, but in our worlds, that would mean death.

For my wife's and her siblings' sake, we would try to keep things civil.

Taking in the people present, I couldn't help but think about my father, the former capo dei capi. Vincent Luciano was no doubt rolling over in his grave. Fuck that. He was clawing his fingers bloody trying to escape the ravages of hell to deliver damnation to me for not only continuing but also nurturing the alliance with the Roríguez cartel.

"Traveling in the States..." Aléjandro began, "...is difficult." He looked at me. "Not only with your government but also with Herrera's men. They're watching."

Dante stiffened at my side at the mention of Elizondro Herrera—our common enemy.

"Are you prepared to answer for Jorge?" I asked.

Aléjandro inhaled, straining the buttons on his shirt and bringing to life tendons and veins in his neck below his tawny skin. "For now. When he arrives, we'll make final decisions."

My brother-in-law's expression emanated power and determination, the same resolution as his brother, Reinaldo, and my other brother-in-law, my wife's brother, Emiliano, displayed.

"Dante," I prompted, "bring everyone up-to-date on the Herrera cartel's activities."

He shifted, widening his stance and clutching his own hand in front of him. "As everyone here knows, in the last three months since Camila's abduction, we've had eyes, ears, and most importantly, technology surveilling the senior officers in Herrera's cartel." He nodded toward Aléjandro. "I've kept you informed of their activities."

Aléjandro nodded. "We have men on the inside. Unfortunately, they aren't privy to information on the drug lord himself."

Dante went on. "For the sake of everyone present, I'll recap. From what we've been able to determine, Elizondro Herrera is still holed up in Mexico. He's sent his men to the States. Their primary goal is to cause disruptions with the famiglia and Roríguez cartel. We believe he wants to make both organizations appear incompetent and weak."

Carmine's stance straightened, and Salvatore's jaws clenched.

Since my ascension to capo dei capi, my uncles have managed to keep their disagreements with my decisions private. We're family and they have my back, but that doesn't mean they're happy about it.

"Wanderland was raided," Emiliano said, speaking of the cartel's private club near San Diego. "The feds seized cash, but no drugs were found." He turned to Aléjandro. "We were given advance notice by an informant. Since the whores have been living at the renovated school, Mia's worked to ensure that each worker has the necessary paperwork. She's tracked down birth certificates and encouraged those without an education to complete their GED. My uncle was worried this would encourage them to leave, but it's done the opposite. They're more content. I even heard a few talking about saving money. Every one of the whores interviewed passed the feds' interrogation with flying colors." He shook his head. "Besides confiscating a few Gs in cash, the feds walked away disappointed."

My mind filled with problems we'd encountered at Emerald Club in Kansas City. It was the famiglia's business similar to Wanderland. Our establishment catered to a higher clientele with our VIP lounges, but both clubs had alcohol, drugs, and sex on the menu.

"The bratvas," I prompted.

"Goal number two," Dante responded. "Lorenzo, our tech man, has captured communication between Herrera and Volkov."

Everyone nodded in agreement. Volkov ran the bratva on the West Coast. We'd known about their alliance for a while. The next bit of news would come as more of a shock.

"Herrera is also in contact with Myshkin," Dante paused before adding, "the pakhan here in Kansas City and St. Louis."

Aléjandro's eyes widened. "You confirmed this information?"

"Yes," I replied. "We just got the confirmation yesterday. I spoke to Myshkin myself."

"Why?" Andrés said, suddenly coming to attention. "You think he'd tell you the truth?"

"I wasn't sure. We made a deal."

Aléjandro stood. "A deal with the bratva. You can't trust them."

I half grinned. "The same has been said about the cartel."

"Dealing with the bratva makes the famiglia compromised," Andrés said, his voice growing louder and his cheeks reddening. "We can't risk two associations—"

Aléjandro lifted his hand, silencing Andrés. The old man may have stopped talking, but Aléjandro's wordless command didn't stop the crimson from growing brighter on Andrés's neck and face. "What deal?" he asked me.

"I asked for information on Herrera."

Aléjandro's nostrils flared. "He had it?"

"He did." My words were measured and calm. "I proposed a truce. The fighting between the famiglia and bratva is becoming a no-win for either side. If I agree to certain conditions, Myshkin and I believe we can work together to take out Herrera and Volkov."

Aléjandro asked, "You enter into an alliance with Myshkin, what does that mean for us—the Roriguez cartel?"

"We're still negotiating."

"If he agreed to help you, you made some deal," Aléjandro said.

"I did." I inhaled. "As far as Myshkin's territory here in Kansas City, we agreed on boundaries, stop the bloodshed on the streets."

"And you went along?"

I shook my head. "No."

"The fuck?" Andrés cursed.

"As I said, we're still negotiating." I nodded. "Once it's done, we all benefit."

"We can win this war," Aléjandro said. "We will win." Each phrase was louder than the last.

"We'll get rid of Herrera for good," I said. "Can we count on you?"

Aléjandro inhaled. "*Sí. Nosotros somos familia.*"

"With Myshkin, Roríguez, and the famiglia, we will win."

We all turned toward the door at the sound of a knock. Each man instinctively reached for his weapon.

"No need," I said. "Our soldiers are out there. No threat would make it to my door." I raised my voice. "Enter."

"*Feliz Navidad,*" Jorge Roríguez greeted as he entered, followed by Nicolas Ruiz, Andrés's brother, and Nick, Nicolas's son.

"Welcome to our home."

Jorge came straight to me and shook my hand. "Do they know?"

"Yes, I just told them."

He turned toward the rest of the room. "Tonight, we'll celebrate with our growing family." He laid a large hand on my shoulder. "All our family. *Siete peces.* Tomorrow, we strategize. We have a war to win."

Aléjandro was the first to respond. "*Papá,* you knew about Myshkin?"

Jorge nodded. "How did you respond?"

"Capo and Dante are family. The famiglia is our family. I responded that we are one."

Jorge's cheeks rose in a smile. "*Mi hijo. Estas listo.*"

Andrés bristled as Aléjandro replied, "I have more to learn."

I gestured toward the door. "This discussion stays in this room. The women don't need to worry." Everyone nodded. "Now, let's celebrate before we take care of business."

Dante remained at my side as the others filtered out of the office. "Thoughts?" he asked.

My forehead furrowed. "Jorge seemed pleased with Aléjandro. You know them better than I do. Thoughts on Reinaldo and Emiliano?"

Dante inhaled. "I thought Jasmine wasn't an option."

A scoff escaped my lips as I shook my head. "Who said anything about Jasmine?"

"You've been making deals. Jorge wasn't upset about you involving Myshkin."

"Jorge wants to defeat Herrera."

Dante lowered his voice. "He also wants Rei married. He's pushing Jano to make more decisions. If you ask me, he's securing his legacy—his family."

"Jasmine isn't a Luciano," I replied.

"I'm not blind and neither are you. Jasmine is beautiful, sweet, and smart. If Rei wants her, after what I did, it could help cement this alliance."

"This alliance is cemented," I growled. "We have a war to fight, one we have to win. Besides, Rei isn't the only one with an interest in Jasmine." I could hardly make myself force out the words. "Myshkin wants her for his son, Zhdan."

"Fuck," Dante murmured. "You can't send her off to the bratva"

"We need a ceasefire with Myshkin."

Jasmine
The night before

My knees tucked beneath my robe, I hugged them to my chest as I leaned back against the window seat wall in my bedroom and stared through the frosty panes. Snow fell steadily from the dark sky. Stories below, the sidewalks were growing less distinguishable, their surfaces and the grass becoming one, hidden beneath a blanket of fresh accumulation. Illumination from the streetlights sparkled on the wet and slick streets like holiday lights.

I held the small kitten, keeping her cuddled against my skin.

Warm within my cocoon, my memories warred between the life I mostly recalled and that which was beyond my recollection. There was something magical, or perhaps tragic, about the first snowfall of the season that surfaced bits and pieces of memories buried deep within the recesses of my mind.

Despite my luxurious surroundings, my fingers and toes ached from phantom cold, a deep-seated chill that couldn't be warmed. When I was young, I used to wake on the night of the first snow to fears I found impossible to articulate. I would make my way to the bedroom next door to wake my sister, Josie. She'd take me back to my room and climb into bed with me, telling me that we were now warm and safe.

No matter how difficult my questions or how many I could produce, Josie patiently answered each one. She recounted the time after we lost our grandparents when it was the two of us against the world. There were nights spent wrapped in blankets in her old car and mornings spent at a truck stop to shower before school. Rarely did she discuss our mother. I knew the subject wasn't one Josie liked to remember. We went to live with our grandparents after our mother was convicted of manslaughter in a drug deal gone bad and sentenced to twenty years in prison. Until our grandparents died in a car crash, we had a decent home for the first time in our lives.

As time passed and I grew into adulthood, I became uncertain if the memories I recalled were my own or those given to me through Josie's stories. The fact that my hands and feet were numb despite the tempered glass and abundant heat was evidence that the past still lurked in my subconscious.

Tipping my forehead to my knees, I let out a sigh.

My mind knew that I'd never again suffer as we had

before moving in with Dario Luciano. He'd taken us both under his protective wing. Even today, years after my sister was stolen from us, Dario was here for me, supporting me, and providing for me. His influence couldn't be understated.

Dario was first and foremost the capo dei capi of Kansas City. He was also a man of strong beliefs. While his family disapproved of him bringing me and Josie into his home, he was a man of his word—and was to this day.

He was also a collector of fine things.

Dario's influence was evident in my choice of twin majors at Barnard College in New York: history, particularly the Renaissance, and archaeology. I was currently on semester break of my sophomore year. While I thought I'd enjoy the freedom of a college campus, I'd yet to experience any. As Dario Luciano's responsibility, even at the age of twenty years old, I had my bodyguard to protect me at all times.

It wasn't easy fitting into the student life with a large and intimidating man constantly in my shadow. While I longed for a regular life with freedom of choice, I was caged by the awful memories of what life could be like without Dario's overprotective influence.

I laid the sleeping kitten on the blanket and quietly exited my bedroom. The stillness of the night buzzed in my ears, sending my senses into overdrive. I'd walked these hallways since I was seven years old, knowing each turn and what was behind every door. The simple life we'd had when I was a child was now replaced with more.

More people.

More noise.

More responsibilities.

It wasn't only that in the last few years Dario had become the capo dei capi of the Kansas City Famiglia, making his office on the first floor a place for meetings that brought dangerous people into our home. The last few years had also brought Catalina, Dario's wife, and Ariadna Gia, their beautiful daughter, into our fold. Dario's marriage was the fruition of an alliance between the Kansas City Famiglia and the Roríguez cartel.

The dangers I'd been raised to avoid were present at every turn.

At first, I had my doubts about their arranged marriage, but Catalina was a great match for Dario. Her open and loving heart balanced Dario's more reserved personality, making us a family. Because of that bond, tomorrow our home would be filled with members of the Kansas City Famiglia and the Roriguez cartel, including *el Patrón* himself.

I shivered at the thought.

Making my way down the staircase to the first floor, I quietly entered the kitchen. I expected to find one of our bodyguards, Armando or Piero, keeping watch. To my surprise, the kitchen was empty, the hum of the refrigerators and lingering aromas of Contessa's cooking in preparation for tomorrow night's feast filling the dimly lit room.

The light from within the refrigerator was blinding as I reached for a water bottle. The clock on the microwave told me that it was past midnight, officially

Christmas Eve. I couldn't pinpoint why I wasn't tired, but I wasn't.

Perhaps I needed to push away my fears of the first snow.

My bare feet padded down the hallway toward the living room. The floor-to-ceiling windows beckoned me closer like a giant movie screen of the season's first snow. The city lights combined with the ambient light and white falling snow cast a gray illumination throughout the room.

Taking a drink of my water, I spun to a noise. Almost choking with my pulse now racing, I saw a man I didn't know standing before me.

"Who are you?" The wavering in my voice threatened to give away my unease. The small hairs on my neck rose to attention and goose bumps materialized beneath my pajamas. This was my home.

Why is he here?

Quickly, my gaze darted around the room, searching for Piero or Armando. My thoughts were fragments trying to make sense of his presence. There was something about this man, an air of danger and power. Muscles with tattoos bulged from beneath the sleeve of his dark t-shirt. While there was a holster over one shoulder, this man didn't need weapons: he could maim or kill with his hands.

I'd heard Catalina's brother was visiting for the holiday. I knew Em. This wasn't him.

Despite my recent drink, my mouth went dry as the man walked toward me, each step of his boots echoing on the marble tile. His jean-clad long legs reached me in a few steps. With the closeness came a better view of his handsome face, prominent brow, and defined jaw covered by a trimmed beard. His chest seemed wider, and his height dwarfed mine.

His dark hair was short on the sides and longer on top. The scent of sandalwood and leather permeated my senses. Securing the cap on my water bottle, I set it on the windowsill. Straightening my neck, I stood tall, feigning strength, as I tried to put together the pieces. "You're from the Roríguez cartel." It wasn't a question and at the same time, it was.

"*Sí.*"

Was he one of their guards? A soldier wouldn't move with the confidence he emanated. The way he moved was graceful as if he'd choreographed a dance—perhaps a tango. No, I was wrong. His steps were predatory, a lion approaching his prey.

I took a step back.

He was close enough that I had to raise my chin to maintain my view of his almost fully black orbs. Another step and I would collide with the cool glass of the window. I held my ground

"You're Jasmine."

He pronounced my name in a way I'd never heard. *Jazz-mean.*

I nodded.

His lips curled, yet his black stare wasn't smiling.

I sucked in a breath and flinched as his hand came upward, twisting and running a ringlet of my hair through his fingers. "They told me you were beautiful."

He tilted his head to the side. "Beautiful doesn't begin to describe you."

Words failed me. There was something about this man that stirred emotions within me in a way I'd never experienced. While at the same time, part of my brain told me to scream and yell, to get away from him.

"You're stunning." He nodded. "You've grown up since the capo's wedding." His gaze was on my hair. "I've never seen such red hair." His gaze returned to mine as his hand fell to his side. "Or blue eyes."

Bravely, I lifted my hand to his chest. "Stop." Despite his calm exterior, beneath my touch, this man's heart too was racing, thumping wildly. Energy pulsated from him to me as if our touch was a conduit for electricity. I met his gaze. "Tell me who you are and how you're here in my home."

"You do not recognize me?" He took a step back and bowed at the waist before standing erect. "*Lo lament. Mí nombre es* Reinaldo. Some call me Rei."

My mind searched for the mention of him. He was present at Dario's wedding.

"Perhaps you've heard of *mí padre*, Jorge Roríguez."

Oh. The connection was made. I'd attended Dario's wedding as this man's brother's plus-one. "You're *el Patrón's* son and Aléjandro's brother?"

Rei nodded before cupping my chin and running his thumb over my cheek. "Your skin is like glass." His touch against my flesh was like the striking of a match, his thumb rough and callused, lighting a flame within me. My panties dampened and my nipples beaded.

"Please," I said, less strong than I would have preferred. "You shouldn't be touching me."

He glanced down at my breasts, and his smile returned.

Why hadn't I secured my robe?

I backed up as he took one more step toward me, and my shoulders collided with the cool windowpane. His massive body was millimeters away. If I so much as inhaled deeply, my breasts would meet his broad chest.

His dark eyes hooded, and his nostrils flared. "Tell me, Jasmine. Has a man ever touched you before, brought you pleasure?"

"I really think you should back up." I inhaled. "If one of my bodyguards sees you..."

"I could gut him before he drew his weapon." Rei again reached for my chin and ran that same thumb over my lips. "You would like it...if I touched you."

Words failed me. I was too busy fighting whatever spell he'd cast. My body and mind battled. My body wanted to inhale, to feel his hard body against mine and to experience what he described. My mind was busy telling me to run from his threat.

Rei's timbre dropped an octave. "Even now" —his thumb moved slowly— "your breathing has become shallower, and here" —he moved his touch to my neck— "your vein is pulsating. Your nipples have grown harder beneath that top. I might scare you, but you've lived with the capo dei capi. Danger also excites you."

"I don't know what you're talking about. I'm not scared," I lied.

His lips twitched as if a smile was close to morphing

his granite features as he lowered his touch down the side of my neck and collarbone. "You're brave. I admire a woman who doesn't cower."

I wanted to tell him again not to touch me, but that same touch caused my circulation to quicken, my insides to twist, and my brain to forget how to form words.

"Soon, you will know what I mean."

I shook my head. "I don't understand."

Rei took a step back. He reached for my hand and again bowed, this time leaving a kiss on my knuckles. "It was a pleasure to formally meet you, Jasmine." He turned and walked toward the staircase.

The son of the drug lord of the Roríguez cartel was staying in my house.

I waited until he disappeared before I let out the breath I'd been holding. Fear was an interesting emotion. All my life I'd been told to avoid danger, to stay safe. There was nothing safe about Reinaldo Roríguez, yet I couldn't decide to keep my distance.

TWO

Jasmine

After that encounter, sleep was out of the question.

My heartbeat was erratic. Goose bumps prickled my flesh, yet I was suddenly warm. There was one place I enjoyed going when I couldn't sleep.

A long time ago, Dario changed one of the rooms on the first floor from a sitting room to a theater room. I couldn't begin to estimate the number of afternoons and late nights I'd spent in the comfy large recliners. Possible titles of favorite movies raced through my thoughts as I opened the door and flipped the switch.

The room filled with ambient lighting, the kind that can be illuminated while a movie or TV show played without distracting from the screen. I didn't need brighter lighting. I knew this room like the back of my hand.

While others enjoyed Hallmark kind of movies around this time of year, my preference was for the less traditional holiday movies such as the old titles *Die Hard* and *Lethal Weapon*. As could be guessed by their titles, these movies had loud soundtracks. Instead of waking the entire apartment—Catalina's parents were staying on the second floor and more of her family was expected soon—I placed the earbuds in my ears and hit the play button on the remote control.

Settling back with a blanket, I watched a movie I'd seen more times than I could count. The repeated gunshots reverberating in my ears could be blamed for my inability to hear the opening of the theater room door. My attention to the screen could be why I didn't notice the movement to my side.

The intensity of the storyline might be the reason I screamed.

A handsome profile appeared in front of the screen. My fingers went to my lips, silencing my scream as my heart raced.

Has Rei found me?

As the light hit his handsome face, I recognized Catalina's brother, Em. I didn't expect his arrival until sometime during the coming day.

He spoke, but I couldn't hear him.

Shaking my head I plucked the earbuds from my ears.

His deep timbre ricocheted through me. "I saw the

light beneath the door." He shook his head. "I didn't mean to frighten you, Jasmine."

"I'm not frightened." I lied. Feigning strength seemed to be my go-to story. "The movie was just really intense."

Emiliano Ruiz turned and looked up at the screen. His smile broadened as he swiveled back toward me. "If machine guns are your holiday fare, you're in the right family." He stepped closer and pointed to the seat at my side. "Do you mind?"

I shook my head and gestured toward it.

He offered me his hand. "It's been a while since I've seen you. I was hoping you'd be home for the holidays." His long fingers encased mine. There was a spark to his touch as if energy flowed through him to me. My breathing shallowed.

There was a familiarity with Em that wasn't the same as Rei. My tension eased.

Em bowed at the waist, lowering his face, and kissing the knuckles of the hand he was still holding. His firm lips sent more sparks through my circulation that only multiplied with the intensity in his gaze.

I retrieved my hand, still sensing his kiss. "I'm on semester break."

Emiliano lowered himself to the seat at my side. He'd changed since the last time I saw him. His body was bulkier and impossibly more toned. His long legs folded as he leaned back, looking at the screen. A blended, intoxicating aroma of spice filled the air. "How many times have you seen this movie?"

My cheeks rose in a grin as I took in his profile,

protruding forehead, high cheekbones, and defined jaw. My mouth grew dry as I answered. "Too many to count."

I sat back, but as I began to place the earbuds in my ears, I realized the problem. "Um, you can't hear without the earbuds. I didn't want to wake the whole house."

"Machine guns, right."

I suddenly wished I'd remembered my Bluetooth earbuds, but they were upstairs in my room. Instead, I had a corded old pair that plugged into the arm of the chair. "We could share." I offered him one of the earbuds and placed the other one in my ear closest to him.

Em placed the earbud in his ear.

Despite all the chaos breaking loose on the screen, I wasn't concentrating on the movie. Leaning closer, so as not to dislodge the earbud, I found myself staring at the arm on our shared armrest. Em was wearing a dark t-shirt, leaving his biceps and forearms exposed. It took every ounce of my self-control to not run my fingers over his defined muscles. Maybe my encounter with Rei had my hormones in overdrive.

He leaned closer. "I thought you were always followed."

"Followed?"

"Bodyguards. I've watched you."

He had?

I cleared my throat. "Dario is a bit overprotective."

Em nodded. "With my sister too." His eyebrows rose. "He has good reason to be with you. You stand out among the others."

My breathing hitched as he reached for a strand of

my hair. "Your fire-colored hair and blue eyes are beacons among the other women."

Is this real?

How did I have a similar conversation with two men in one night?

"You're stunning, Jasmine. I'm sure you know that."

There was something about Em that returned my thoughts to the first snow. Unwanted tears filled my eyes. "My sister used to say I was pretty. But it's been years since I've heard her voice."

Compassion shone in his gaze. "I'm sorry. Is she...?"

Swallowing the unwelcome emotions, I nodded. "I was just thinking about her."

Em's hand came to my cheek, his thumb gently wiping away my tear. "It wasn't my intention to make you cry."

Inhaling, I shook my head and feigned a smile. "Holidays and snow." I shrugged.

"Well, you're beautiful. You should be told every day."

Warmth filled my cheeks. "Thank you."

"Tell me," he said, "how would he feel about me here now?"

"He?" My thoughts went back to Rei. But that wasn't who... "Oh, you mean Dario?"

"*Sí*, capo dei capi."

He wouldn't approve, but I didn't want to say that and risk Em leaving. Instead, I shrugged. "We're just watching a movie."

"That's what we're doing. However, I want to do

something else, something I was told you wouldn't allow Jano to do when he took you to the wedding."

My chest grew tight.

A kiss.

Aléjandro had tried to kiss me that night and Mia intervened. Kisses were supposed to be saved for your husband, that's what Contessa, our housekeeper, told me. I did a good job of following the rules. Those rules kept me safe, kept Dario happy, and gave me a home.

However, I'd thought about Aléjandro's almost-kiss many times. I wasn't attracted to him, not like Em or even Rei. Nevertheless, I wondered what it would be like to be kissed, really kissed, the way they do in books and movies.

After all, it was just a kiss.

Right?

My tongue darted to my lips. "I'm older than I was then."

His lips quirked. "More experienced?"

"No," I replied honestly.

His hand was back to my face, his palm cupping my cheek. "I'm afraid the capo would not approve."

"Do you always strive to please the bosses?" I wasn't sure what was making me say anything to encourage him, other than the way my body suddenly warmed. I leaned closer, my robe-covered breasts rubbing against his strong arm.

"Not always." His timbre was slower and deeper.

My core twisted and my nipples hardened with need. "Good." My reply was barely audible.

Fire burned in his dark orbs as he wove his fingers

through my hair and tugged me closer until our lips met. His kiss was light at first, testing the waters. He tasted of liquor. I wasn't experienced enough to know what kind of liquor, only that in combination with cologne, his strong lips, and his touch of my face and hair, the concoction was intoxicating. I pressed forward, lifting myself higher onto my knees and leaning over the armrest. My touch of his rock-hard broad shoulder was only to steady myself as our kiss took on new life.

His hand moved from my hair to the back of my neck as my body ignited with his kiss.

We both startled at the sound of the door opening and bouncing off the wall.

"Jasmine?"

I sucked in a breath, settling down in my chair and brought my hand to my lips. "Piero," I answered my bodyguard.

He came forward, his gun in his hand. Piero's eyes narrowed as he took in Emiliano. He returned his attention to me. "Armando reported a scream."

"Um, it was the movie. Very suspenseful."

My bodyguard's nostrils flared as he nodded. "It's late—or early. I should see you safely to your room. The house is full of guests."

Standing, I straightened my robe and allowed the blanket to fall to the floor. "That's probably a good idea." I turned to Em. "Good night."

He stood and reached for my hand, a brazen move in front of my armed bodyguard. "Good night, Jasmine. Thank you."

"For?"

He winked. "Just thank you."

More warmth climbed from my chest to my cheeks. "Thank you." I took one last look over my shoulder at the man with whom I'd shared my first kiss before walking away with Piero.

My bodyguard stopped. "Mr. Ruiz, I'll come back and turn off the movie. Feel free to make your way to your room."

Em nodded. "It's late—or early."

As Piero and I walked up the staircase, I whispered, "Could we please keep this between us?"

His jaw clenched.

"We don't want to cause problems between the famiglia and the cartel," I reasoned.

"That's good advice. We should both listen."

I would listen, but it would be impossible for me to forget that kiss. I could still feel his lips and his touch as I turned off the lights and slid under the covers.

CHAPTER

THREE

Jasmine

Christmas Eve in our home was more tradition than a religious celebration. For most of my life, this night was filled with delicious food and our small family. Where there were only four, including Contessa, tonight there were multitudes. It was as if the Bible story of Jesus and the fishes was coming to life. There were currently over twenty people to be fed. With bodyguards, the number rose to over forty.

Savory aromas filled the kitchen as Contessa managed multiple tasks. She wasn't alone: Arianna Luciano brought her cook Greta along to help. Heaven forbid, Dario's mother would actually do something as mundane as culinary activities. No, she was busy spending as much time with her granddaughter as possible.

The granddaughter wasn't me.

I wasn't a Luciano. While I'd lived with Dario since I was seven, the Luciano famiglia beyond Dario and Dante liked to pretend I didn't exist.

While that hadn't exactly changed, I existed, and I now had a powerful ally, not that Dario as capo dei capi of Kansas City wasn't powerful. Catalina was on my side, more than supportive once she learned about me. As the mother of the aforementioned granddaughter, her opinion carried a lot of weight with Mrs. Arianna Luciano.

"I've never seen this dining room table so long," I said as I helped Catalina arrange the water goblets at each place setting.

"Contessa has the whole seven-fishes menu down to a science." Catalina questioned, "Dario didn't invite his family here for Christmas Eve when you were young?"

My mind went back to my childhood. "Neither Mrs. Luciano nor the capo, Dario's father, would come to the apartment after my sister and I moved in. They hosted a large celebration at the big house in the Ozarks, but we weren't invited. Dario wouldn't go. It was just us."

Catalina came closer and wrapped her arm around my shoulders. "Now, they're all coming to *your* home, including Arianna."

I scanned the table, set for nearly thirty. "They're not all happy about it," I whispered, thinking about Dario's uncles Carmine and Salvatore. They'd rather starve than break bread with members of the cartel, including

Catalina. Their opinions weren't swayed by a small baby.

She smiled knowingly. "They don't have to be happy. Dario makes the rules. He's determined to make the alliance work, and to work, we need to be one family." She lowered her voice. "You're probably thinking of certain uncles. Truth be told, my uncle Nicolas isn't thrilled about the famiglia. We can ignore them and show them how wrong they are. I'm glad you're open to my family."

"To Dario's family, my opinion doesn't matter."

"You are Dario's family," Catalina said. "And your opinion matters to me. I hope you don't mind that my parents, Em, and Rei are all staying here."

My lips tingled at the mention of the two men. "Your mother is nice." I felt my cheeks warm.

Catalina's eyebrows rose. "Em and Rei?"

I'd seen both of them again this morning, as Dante gave Camila the kitten. "They're cute" —I thought of Rei — "and intense."

She laughed. "Cute? I bet they've never been called that before. Intense is a good description."

"Okay, ruggedly handsome." I shrugged. "You've probably figured out that Dario is a bit overprotective. I've not had a lot of opportunity around men except for bodyguards. I guess I feel different around them."

She scanned me up and down. "Be yourself, Jasmine. Yes, I've noticed his overprotectiveness. It's because he loves you. I expect he'll be the same with Ariadna Gia when men start to notice her."

"Oh God. He'll put her in a convent."

Catalina laughed.

My stomach twisted as I wondered if Piero mentioned what happened last night. "I'm not sure that they notice me?" Yes, after last night I was fishing.

"They do," she exclaimed. "I'm a little afraid Dario will pull one of his knives on them. Surely, you've noticed."

I had.

Having the attention of one of the two was flattering. Having the attention of both was unbelievable.

"You're stunning. You've grown up since the capo's wedding."

"You're beautiful. You should be told every day."

Rei's and Em's words came back to me. Before I could answer, Contessa came into the dining room carrying trays of shrimp cocktail over beds of ice cubes.

"The men are out of their meeting," she announced.

"Do you need any last-minute help?" Catalina asked.

"No, thank you," Contessa replied confidently. "Everyone is in the living room. Mrs. Ruiz is still holding Ariadna Gia."

Catalina's eyes opened wide. "Oh, Arianna isn't happy."

"You may want to intervene."

"I can help you, Contessa," I volunteered as Catalina hurried away.

Contessa's loving gray eyes settled on me. "I appreciate you." She lifted her chin. "Go out there with everyone and show them that you belong here."

"Do I?"

"More than anyone. This is your home and has been

for over thirteen years. Don't let last names stand in your way, Jasmine. If Mr. Luciano's family can accept the cartel, they can accept you. They should have done so a long time ago. Show them they've been wrong."

Smoothing my dress, I lifted my chin and walked toward the voices. Truth be told, I was more comfortable around Catalina's family than Dario's. At least her family hadn't snubbed me for the last fourteen years. Since Catalina and Dario wed and Catalina welcomed me in their home, his family now speaks to me.

A fire crackled in the fireplace as holiday music filled the air. In the corner near the windows was a lighted tree that nearly reached the ceiling, fourteen feet high. I grinned as Catalina took her daughter from her mother's arms, claiming that the baby was in need of a diaper change before dinner.

As I scanned the room, I couldn't help but think about Dario's goal for one family. With a few exceptions, the room was divided into small groupings of like-minded people. The cartel women were mostly gathered together. Josefina Roríguez was seated at Valentina's side. It was difficult to believe Josefina was Aléjandro and Reinaldo's mother, as she looked too young and beautiful to be the mother of grown men. Also, the famiglia women were congregated, the exception being those gathered around Ariadna Gia.

Carmine Luciano and Salvatore Luciano, Dario's uncles, stood guard over their respective families, no doubt not wanting their sons or daughters interacting with the cartel. I hadn't seen Salvatore's daughter, Isabella, since Dario's wedding. She wasn't a little girl any longer. If Carmine had his way, my guess was that he'd rather have her in a convent than in the presence of cartel men.

Another exception was Mia and Camila seated together with their husbands attentively at their sides. Mia's baby bump was more than a bump, and Aléjandro was beaming at her side.

"It's difficult...deciding which team to cheer for?"

I turned to the deep voice, coming face-to-face with the handsome man who last night gave me my first real kiss. Emiliano Ruiz. "According to Dario, we're all one team."

"It's not often you meet a capo who's also a dreamer."

A smile curled my lips. "You don't think it's possible?"

He shrugged his wide shoulders as his dark stare scanned the room. "I think it's possible, but shaky." He lowered his voice. "I hope I didn't get you in trouble last night."

Meeting his gaze, I shook my head. "Piero will keep our secret."

"What if I kissed you here and now?"

My eyes opened wider. "Let's not test that theory."

His lips quirked into a sexy grin as he nodded toward the highboy. "Are you a red or white wine lady?"

"White goes best with fish. I like sweet wines."

The temperature of the room spiked, and I sucked in a breath as Emiliano placed his hand in the small of my back.

"Come with me and I'll pour you a glass, and you can explain this seven-fishes thing to me."

Trying to ignore the way his touch sent a tingling sensation through me, I found my voice. "It's an Italian-American thing. Tradition..." As we crossed the room, I caught Dario staring in our direction.

Overprotective was an understatement.

Is he armed?

Of course he was.

At the highboy, as I continued on about the Christmas Eve tradition, Reinaldo joined us. Suddenly, I was surrounded by two rock-hard bodies. Unlike Dario who always wore a suit, Reinaldo and Emiliano were both dressed in black jeans and button-up shirts. Reinaldo's was white with the sleeves rolled up showing off his powerful forearms and the fringe of a tattoo. Emiliano's was light blue. Instead of the boots they often wear, both men were wearing expensive leather loafers. They both wore gold chains around their necks. Their warmth encompassed me as the spicy scent of their cologne filled my senses.

"I see the two of you know one another." Rei's stare was intense.

"We met when Cat married the capo." Em looked at me and grinned. "Would that make you my step-niece?"

Warmth filled my cheeks. "I don't think that's how it works. Dario isn't my father, and Catalina isn't my stepmother."

Having the two men together, I could not only sense their different personalities but hear them as well. Emiliano's accent was barely noticeable compared to Reinaldo's, probably the result of the former living his entire life in California.

"You never mentioned Jasmine," Rei said to Em, using the strange pronunciation of my name.

Em stood taller after handing me a glass of moscato. "Have you two met?" He turned to me. "Jasmine, this is Rei, Reinaldo Roríguez." He turned to Rei. "Rei, this is Jasmine."

Rei's penetrating dark gaze was locked on me. "We met...last night."

The intensity of his stare brought back the feelings from last night, the almost painful twisting of my insides. I said a prayer that my padded bra was keeping my nipples from giving me away.

Emiliano quickly poured himself a glass of cabernet and lifted it to me. "Cheers." He looked at Reinaldo and back to me. "I have an idea. We're planning an escape for later tonight. Jasmine should join us."

"Where do you think you can escape to on Christmas Eve?" I asked.

"Emerald Club is open," Em replied.

I nearly spit out my wine. "Oh, I'm most certain that Dario wouldn't approve."

"You're an adult," Rei said. He lifted his dark eyebrows. "Aren't you? You don't need Daddy's permission."

"I am an adult." I recently turned twenty and Dario wasn't my dad. He was my guardian, but that will be legally revoked upon my next birthday. "But seriously, Emerald Club? As soon as we stepped through the doors, one of the guards would call Dario."

"There has to be someplace in this city that is more exciting than here," Em said.

We all turned toward the large room.

"This is exciting," Rei said. "We can guess who will pull out the first weapon."

"See that man over there, the one looking our direction?" I asked.

They both hummed their response.

"That's Piero, my bodyguard."

"We've met," Em said, lowering his voice. "The way he's staring at us, he may be the first one to pull out his gun."

"I'd gut him before he had the chance," Rei said in a menacing murmur.

"Excuse me," Contessa said over the din of voices. "First course is served."

People around the room began to stand and move toward the dining room.

"Are there assigned seats?" Em asked.

"Dario is at one end," I replied. "And *el Patrón* at the other."

Em leaned down, whispering near my ear. "Tell Piero to take the night off. Rei and I will keep you safe."

Emiliano pulled out my chair and helped me sit before the two of them sat on either side of me. The warmth of their legs pressed against mine beneath the table gave me a feeling that was the opposite of safe. It stirred a fire within me, tending the flames I'd felt for both of them since last night.

Somehow, we managed our way through all five courses.

I'd grown up with this tradition and knew how to take it easy with the first few courses as the food continued to come. It was clear that many from the cartel weren't as familiar. They'd eaten too much in the beginning and as Contessa announced dessert, there were many groans and the murmurs of being too full.

As people were stepping away from the table, Em leaned closer to me. "Are you ready to get out of here?"

I turned to Rei. "Do you want me to go?"

He shrugged. "If you can get away from your bodyguard."

CHAPTER
FOUR

Reinaldo

Jasmine's blue eyes opened wide as she looked from me to Em and around the room. In our few meetings, it was becoming clear why *mí padre* mentioned her to me. Her beauty was unique. I'd had a difficult time, even in the meeting with the capo, thinking of anything other than last night's encounter, the way her body responded to me. Taking her out into the city didn't sit well with me. Nothing since I found her with Em had sat well with me. He was my friend and *mí padre's* soldier, but if he continued to put his hands on Jasmine, I would need to cut them off. The announcement that she was to be mine was supposed to wait. Dario Luciano had not fully agreed. There was more negotiation.

"No one's watching," Em said. "They won't even notice."

A sad shadow swept over her beautiful face. "You're probably right."

I was good at many things and extremely good at others. Give me a problem and I could navigate the web, light and dark. I could find answers to questions people didn't even know they had. I was accurate with a gun and deadly with a knife. I'd never walked away from a battle. Something else I'd learned to do as the second son of the leader of the Roríguez cartel was read people.

Some individuals such as the capo dei capi were more difficult. He excelled at concealing his expressions. Jasmine was by contrast an open book. Last night she was both frightened and turned on. Tonight, she was less scared, yet cautiously leery. The shadow that just passed over her expression was another layer.

Sadness.

What does this gorgeous woman have to be sad about?

Her voice was low. "I should tell Piero."

Em stepped closer, his expression calculating as if he had everything planned. "Tell Piero that you're going up to your room. Let him claim ignorance if we're caught—which we won't be."

She looked up at him, now standing closer than necessary.

He winked with a smirk. "Do you think he'll let you off twice?"

Twice?

Her lips came together in a straight line as she shook her head. "There are cameras in the elevator."

Em rubbed his palm over her arm, awakening a need within me to tug her away from his touch. I clenched my teeth.

"The guards are busy protecting the capo and *el Patrón*," Em said. "They won't notice if we step out for a few hours."

"She doesn't have it in her to rebel," I said. "Look at her. She's a rule follower through and through. She's probably scared to be without her bodyguards." A smirk quirked my lips. "Frightening things can happen when you're out of their sight."

Jasmine lifted her chin and stood taller.

Watching her feign strength was entertaining.

My fascination with Jasmine didn't begin last night. No, she'd been on my radar since Cat's wedding.

My brother, Jano, had done his research. He usually did. That was why he was the right person to take over the cartel when the time came. Although he had a reputation as a hothead, the reality was that Jano strategized. He took the time to get to know his enemies and relished the consequences of hitting them where it hurt. How he found out about Jasmine I never asked.

Once he did, he made his way to New York and learned her routine. After running into her a few times at a coffee shop, he began the conversation. He was invited to a wedding in the Ozarks. Jasmine fell for his lines, and Jano made his unspoken statement to Dario, then the future capo.

Dario's family didn't want Jasmine at the wedding.

Jano brought her.

The cartel would work to make the alliance

successful on our own terms. We didn't answer to the capo dei capi. Of course, that was before Jano married Dario's sister. The threads that bind us were becoming more complex.

With the memories of last night's encounter, I owed a thank-you to my brother. *Mí padre* wanted me to marry Camila. I wasn't against it, but at the same time, I didn't fight for her. As I looked down at this fiery redhead, I believed this time he had the right woman for me.

"I want to go," she said. "Meet me in Dante's apartment in ten minutes."

"Dante's?" Em asked.

She lifted her chin toward the foyer. Two guards stood at each side of the elevator. "We're not going to walk right past them, not together. You two go down first. The doors down there won't be guarded. I'll make up an excuse for going down to his place. We still have the cameras, but if they're not being watched continuously, we might have a chance at the escape."

I hummed approvingly. "Not your first rodeo?"

Jasmine sighed. "My first rodeo, but I've given this possibility a lot of thought over the years. Leaving from Dante and Camila's apartment is our best chance."

"Camila's apartment with Dante," Em said. "You okay with that?"

He was asking me. "We were there this morning to meet the fuzzy cat. She and I are still like we've always been—friends."

"And this" —Jasmine motioned between the three of us— "friends."

She wasn't asking, and while I nodded, the possessiveness I felt was for more than a friend.

With one last look in our direction, Jasmine made her way over to her bodyguard.

"She's hot," Em said, keeping his voice low. "I thought she was a kid when Jano took her to Cat's wedding." His smile grew. "She's grown up."

This was my friend, but at the moment, I wanted to slice the grin from his face. "This was your idea. Where do you think we should take her?"

"If we can get her out of here, my vote is Emerald Club. You know the capo has that place locked down. Don't want anything happening to his princess."

"I'd agree, but Jasmine was right; they'd call the capo and then who knows? *Mí padre* won't be thrilled if we fuck up the alliance."

"Last time I was in Kansas City some of the famiglia guards were talking about a place called Green Lady Lounge—a jazz club." Em pulled out his phone and began swiping. "It's not far and is open until midnight with live music."

"Sounds like a plan." I laid my hand on Em's shoulder. "Nothing happens to Jasmine. Not for the alliance but because she's trusting us. I don't want her to regret that."

"Who the fuck do you think I am?" Em growled.

"No, I mean out there. One of us is with her all the time. She isn't the capo's daughter, but that doesn't mean she's not valuable. That's why he has bodyguards with her 24/7." I tilted my chin. "Let's head down to Dante's place."

The two bodyguards stared into the living room without questioning our intentions. The elevator stopped on the floor below, the doors opening to the same entry we'd seen this morning.

We stepped into the dimly lit apartment. I turned a complete circle. "Nice place."

"Camila would have a nicer home with you."

"Fuck," I growled. A few months ago, I'd been moved to Northern California to oversee our men in that region. *Mí padre* gave me the former lieutenant's giant-ass home. "That damn mansion is too fucking big. I'm ready to move back to your parents' pool house."

"Do you think Dante has any of the good stuff?" Em asked, walking toward the liquor cabinet in the living room.

"He probably just drinks the capo's top shelf."

Em's eyes widened as he pulled out a bottle of Pappy Van Winkle.

"Fuck yeah. Pour me a shot."

Em didn't waste any time, handing me a crystal shot glass filled with amber liquid. "To Jasmine."

Inhaling, I lifted my shot glass until it met Em's. Without hesitation, I threw back the bourbon. The rich blend hit my tongue with vanilla and toasted-wood aromas. A hint of caramel and roasted nuts turned into a spicy finish. Fucking delicious.

We both turned to the sound of the elevator.

My smile disappeared as Jasmine walked off the elevator. Her emerald holiday dress was replaced with tight blue jeans, boots, and a hooded long sweatshirt. Her blue eyes were vibrant, outlined with more makeup than before and her lips were bright, matching her hair. She went from elegant to strikingly sexy. The way those jeans hugged her legs...If anyone else looked at her, I'd have to kill them.

"Sporting a punk look," Em said. "I like it."

Unzipping the sweatshirt, she revealed a sparkly silver top. "Trying not to raise suspicions. I told Camila I'd come down here and check on Diamond." She looked around. "Have you seen her?"

Diamond?

I turned to Em.

"The kitten," he said.

"Oh fuck. I forgot about it. No, we haven't seen it."

Jasmine took off down the hallway.

I lifted my hands. "I'm not going in their bedroom."

A minute later, Jasmine came back with the ball of fluff in her hands. "She was sleeping in her box."

"Safe and sound. Let's go," I said.

"Let me put her back."

When Jasmine returned, her smile was less bright.

"We're not kidnapping you," Em said. "You don't need to look sad."

"I know..."

He reached for her hand, making the small hairs stand on the back of my neck.

"Are you all right?" he asked.

"I've never done anything like this before." Before we could respond, she tilted her head and smiled. "I've wanted to...you two are a bad influence."

"Nothing bad will happen," Em promised. "You have two of the cartel's best soldiers at your service."

Jasmine pulled the hood of her jacket up, hiding her luscious hair. With her eyes downcast, she strolled into the elevator. Em and I stood in front of her, keeping her near the corner and less obvious to the camera. We rode the elevator in silence, thankful that it didn't make any other stops. By the time the elevator made it to the parking garage, we all were ready to bolt. Instead, we walked calmly. I hit the key fob, and the lights flashed on the black Lexus I'd rented yesterday.

"Oh my God," Jasmine exclaimed from the back seat as we closed the doors and started the engine. "We actually did it."

"Time to show you what life can be like when you're not under the capo's thumb," I said. I gritted my teeth and held my breath as in the rearview mirror, I watched Jasmine unzip her hoodie and free her gorgeous fiery mane. Her top sparkled, reflecting the lights from the parking garage and her cheeks had a rosy hue of excitement.

"Where are we headed?" she asked.

"Green Lady Lounge," Em replied.

"Have you heard of it?" I asked.

Biting her lower lip, she shook her head. "I haven't, but that doesn't mean much. Where is it?"

CHAPTER

FIVE

Jasmine

I stared out the windows, viewing the world as I'd never seen it. It was as if the cold air buzzed with electricity, humming with energy. The ground, covered with millions of diamonds, reflected the city lights. Colorful holiday decorations twinkled. From the interstate, I saw the river. The sky radiated the golden illumination lighting the arches over the bridge connecting Missouri and Kansas.

My circulation raced through my veins with a sense of excitement and adventure.

Two years ago, I never would have left my home with the two men in the front seat of this car, especially without Piero or Armando. I'd grown accustomed to my bodyguards' presence. Now their absence was magnified.

Dario claimed the alliance was solid and trustworthy.

He couldn't blame me for believing him and thus trusting Reinaldo and Emiliano.

I didn't want to think about Dario.

My mind filled with the possibilities of an evening out and away from watchful eyes. The two soldiers with me were conversing in a language I didn't speak. A few words here and there made sense but not enough to follow their conversation.

Emiliano turned to me. "The website says that the Green Lady is an exclusive jazz lounge with Kansas City jazz musicians and shows every day of the year."

"And I thought the entire city shut down for Christmas Eve."

Despite Emiliano's information, my skin cooled as the surroundings around us changed. Gone were the shiny towers of the financial district. Decorated trees were replaced by generic tall streetlights. Windows were covered with paper from the inside while others were boarded shut.

"Are you sure this is safe?" I asked.

Emiliano chuckled. "Anyone who approaches us isn't safe. You are safe."

"I don't know about this neighborhood." I ran my palm over my arms.

"We're not far from the Green Lady Lounge," Emiliano said.

I reached for my sweatshirt and tugged it over the sparkly halter top, unsure if I wanted the attention the halter would provide. When I put it on, I was thinking of the two men in the car with me. Our change in scenery was making me reconsider.

Rei parked the car on the street in front of a tall building with a limestone facade.

Looking around, I expected large neon-lit signs, but there were none.

Rei opened my door and offered me his hand.

Sparks rekindled as I laid my palm in his much larger one. "Are you sure about this?" I asked.

"Not even a little bit." His penetrating gaze scanned the street, searching for possible trouble.

"Stay close to me," he said, speaking near my ear and holding tight to my hand. "If for any reason, I'm not with you, stay close to Em."

My gaze went from one to the other. "Okay." I let out a breath. "Let's do this."

The Green Lady Lounge was much smaller than I expected. Of course, Emerald Club was my only standard, and it was mammoth in comparison. A small red canopy over the door had the name of the club. Emiliano opened the glass door.

We were met with a sign saying there was a ten-dollar cover charge. Rei's hand released mine and rested possessively in the small of my back.

I turned to him. "I didn't bring money."

"We have you covered."

Em was the one who paid the cover, peeling bills from his money clip.

The walls inside were painted velvet red. Vintage oil paintings hung from the walls and a colorful variety of lamps, looking like something from a century ago, hung over a massive bar. It was as if we'd stepped back in time. Rei led me to an empty circular booth. I scooted in and each man sat on either side.

All the waiters were dressed in suits and ties and the waitresses in cocktail dresses.

A man with a saxophone was on the main stage beside a large organ and drum set. Music filled the air along with the din of patrons. The eclectic group of customers put my mind a little more at ease. It seemed there were people of all ages, races, and styles.

My sweatshirt felt out of place. Unzipping it, I tugged it off, revealing my halter. Rei's jaw clenched. His concentrated stare scanned over my top with enough intensity to scorch my skin beneath. Each second his eyes roamed was the strike of a match, igniting synapse after synapse until my flesh peppered with goose bumps and my nipples hardened.

"You're stunning," Em said.

My gaze met Rei's. "You don't approve?"

"Just hadn't planned on killing anyone tonight."

"You're joking, right?"

Rei and Em exchanged glances in a way that didn't answer my question.

A blond man at the bar caught my attention. His light blue eyes stared in our direction and his smile seemed sinister, telling me that he was equally as dangerous as the men at my sides.

"Do you know that man?" I asked.

Rei was the one who saw him first. "No, but if he doesn't stop looking at you, I'll make it a point to cut out his eyes."

I shivered at the thought as a waitress appeared at the table, blocking the blond man's view.

"Welcome to Green Lady Lounge. Can I interest you in anything from the bar?"

After she took our orders, I looked around. The man was no longer at the bar, easing my nerves. "I took a modern history course last semester," I said, beginning a new subject. "This place could be a field trip."

I had their attention.

"Tell us more," Em said.

"During Prohibition these types of cocktail lounges were a major part of American social life."

"They were illegal," Rei said.

"Yes," I agreed. "Usually set up and run by criminals like Al Capone."

"The Mafia gets all the good crime stories," Em said.

Reinaldo shook his head. "It's time Jasmine broadens her criminal exposure."

After our drinks arrived, Em laid his hand on my thigh. "How does it feel?"

"Exciting." I didn't try to contain my grin. "Like I was saying, this place is like something out of an old black-and-white movie." I lifted the martini glass. "Down to every detail."

"You could never be in a black-and-white movie," he said.

"I couldn't?"

Em's fingers gently squeezed my thigh. "It wouldn't do you justice. You're far too beautiful and colorful to be monochrome."

Reinaldo's nostrils flared, and the muscles pulled taut in his cheeks.

"There's another stage downstairs," Em said. "Come with me and check it out."

When I started to move, Rei covered my hand with his. "She's staying here."

"I would like to see—"

Rei released my hand and lifted his bourbon. "Check it out and come back," he said to Em. "She's safe sitting here with me."

"Jasmine?" Em asked.

I shook my head. "I'm happy here."

After Em walked away, Rei turned toward me. "Are you?"

"That was my question. Am I safe with you?"

For the first time since we'd left the penthouse, a smile curled his lips. "You're safe from other monsters."

My quickened pulse returned. "Other monsters? Are you a monster? Is Em?"

"We all are. It's how we live another day and how we can live with ourselves when we finally sleep. You're not unaccustomed to monsters. You've lived with one for most of your life." Reinaldo laid his arm on the top of the booth behind me. "I've been thinking about last night."

Warmth filled my cheeks as I released the stem of my glass. "Me too."

"Now that we've been formally introduced, I'd like to get to know you better."

My breathing hitched as I found myself lost in his black orbs. They pulled me in, such as a black hole in space. I was powerless to back away. He reached for my hand, sending electrical current through my circulation. I found it difficult to take a full breath as his warm lips brushed my knuckles.

Silence ensued despite the busy lounge around us. Rei and I were in a bubble of our own. Rei's gape continued. It was as if he looked away for even a millisecond, I might disappear. There was more than black to his eyes. Swirls of emotions lightened the darkness within.

"How much better?" I asked.

"Do you remember my question last night?"

"Not verbatim."

"I asked if any man has ever touched you before, brought you pleasure."

I sucked in a breath. "I remember that."

"You didn't answer me."

"No man has touched me before you last night."

His almost-smile reappeared. "That's what I want, to be the man who touches you, kisses you, and brings you pleasure like you've never dared to imagine."

"I don't know you."

"You know Emiliano?" There was something in his tone that made me uneasy.

"Not well, but I've known him since the wedding. I just met you."

Rei shook his head. "We met at the wedding too. Jano introduced me. I'm apparently not memorable."

A scoff escaped my lips. "That's not true at all. You're very memorable. The wedding was a bit stressful. I wasn't supposed to be there. It's more of a blur."

"I remember you." Again, he reached for a strand of my hair and ran it through his fingers. "You're not easy to forget. But back then, the alliance was just beginning. As you know, it's grown. And there are problems."

It was the most I'd heard him say. "Problems?"

"*Sí*, another cartel wants to take over our outfit." He sat taller. "It won't happen. We're stronger as an alliance." He cupped my cheek.

I leaned toward his warm touch.

"I want to kiss you."

Words were beyond me as I nodded.

Our lips met, stealing my breath. Unlike Em, Rei wasn't soft and tentative. He wasn't testing the waters. No, just like his personality, Rei's kiss was powerful, a race car going from zero to two hundred in the blink of an eye.

I didn't know how he did it. The sensation of his lips wasn't confined to my lips. I felt him everywhere. From the tingling in my toes to awareness in my scalp. Heat flooded my circulation.

His hands left a ghost of a touch over my arms until he cupped the back of my neck. Sparks smoldering within the ashes of last night's encounter ignited within me. I leaned closer, pressing my breasts against his solid chest until I remembered we weren't alone. Pulling away, my lips felt swollen. I looked down, concentrating on the gold chain around his neck.

Rei lifted my chin, bringing our gazes together. "That is how I want to know you better. Only me, Jasmine."

Only him.

My thoughts went to Em.

I pressed my lips together. "I'm certain Dario wouldn't approve."

"He will. I've made up my mind."

Straightening my neck, I met his gaze. "You've made up your mind? What about me?"

A smug smile lifted his cheeks. "Your nipples are hard beneath this top. They were last night too." He lowered his face to my neck and inhaled. "I'd place money that your panties are damp. You smell like the sweetest arousal." He lifted his brow. "That is, if you're wearing them. Tell me if you're wearing panties."

I blinked. "I can't— No one has ever spoken to me—"

"If anyone does, I'll kill them. Only me."

That was the second time he'd said that.

"Your body has told me what your words haven't. Jasmine, you're meant to be mine."

This was moving too fast. "The thing is...I'm not a Luciano, but that doesn't mean I'm easy or I'm less. Dario's rules still apply." Before he could respond, I let my anger be known. "I'm not a Luciano. You're the son of the drug lord. What are you offering, Rei? Maybe I could be your mistress? I know, a piece on the side but not one you bring home to Mom and Dad?"

Reinaldo's phone vibrated and his eyes opened wide as he released my hand. "Fuck no. I didn't intend to insinuate..." He pulled his phone from his pocket and read the screen. His attention came back to me. "I don't give a fuck about your last name, only that because of your relationship with the capo, *mí padre* has agreed to talk to Dario."

"About me?"

His jaw clenched as he disconnected the incoming call and tossed his phone on the table. "*Sí*. He has spoken with the capo. My intentions should be made public before anyone else thinks they have a chance."

This was insane. "I'm not a hot commodity. I'm not Mia, the daughter of the capo. Vincent, Dario's father, wouldn't even speak to me."

"He was an ass. *Mí padre* was leery of him. Dario, he trusts. The current capo dei capi knows your worth. That's why currently, Piero is having his ass chewed."

I scrunched my nose. "I don't want Piero in trouble."

"Those calls were from Jano. We're probably screwed."

Before I could reply, the music stopped, and the patrons clapped. Once the applause quieted, I turned back to Rei. "I don't want to think about what will happen when we get back, but I do think you're wrong about me."

"I'm not."

"Catalina says that Dario wants me to finish my bachelor's degree before I consider marriage."

"Forgive me," he said, "but that was what was said about Camila." Rei took a drink of his bourbon. "And she's married."

"You missed out on her, so you want to put your name on me?" I began to scoot away from him and toward the end of the booth.

Reinaldo reached again for my hand. "Stop."

I looked at his hand and back up to his dark gaze. A moment ago, I wanted to continue our kiss. Now, I wanted to leave. His phone vibrated again on the table.

"Great night, Rei. I'm ready to go home. Maybe I am second class—or second choice."

He shook his head, bringing his face to mine. His words came out as more of a growl. "If we were alone, I'd place you over my knee. Do not put words in my mouth."

Over his knee.

Is he serious?

"I'm not a child to be punished."

"You're not a child. You're being unreasonable."

"Me?" My voice was louder than I intended. "I think you're refusing to face facts. Dario won't let me marry and even if he would, I'm not good enough for you."

Rei closed his eyes and exhaled, his nostrils flaring. "Listen to me. You are neither second class nor second choice. *Mí padre* wanted me to marry Camila. She wasn't my choice. You are."

A cascade of thoughts avalanched through my mind.

"What exactly are you asking?"

"*Mí padre* is currently in negotiations for your hand."

His phone vibrated again on the table.

Rei reached for his phone and turned it off.

Before I could respond, Em appeared before our table. If I didn't know him, his expression and the way his jaw was clenched and tendons pulled tight in his neck would frighten me.

I knew him, and they did.

"*Qué pasó?*" Rei asked.

Emiliano's gaze narrowed. "Is something going on between you two?" He pulled his money clip from his jean pocket, peeled off a hundred-dollar bill, and slapped it on the table. "Tell me in the car. *Vamonos*. We're going."

The next part of the conversation occurred in

Spanish as I scrambled for my sweatshirt and hurried from the booth. Em was the one to place his hand in the small of my back. Tension emanated from both men as they led me through the tables toward the front door.

Out on the street, large snowflakes landed on my hair and eyelashes. I wrapped my sweatshirt around me and asked, "What is it?"

"Myshkin's men," Rei answered.

Myshkin. I'd heard that name, but I didn't know where or when.

"Kansas City bratva," Em said as he rushed me toward the car.

I was almost inside the back seat when the gunshots echoed like firecrackers, and the windows shattered at our side.

CHAPTER

SIX

Reinaldo

"**F**uck," I roared as bullets soared our direction through the falling snow. The windows of the limestone building splintered, raining shards down on the sidewalk. Kneeling behind the rental car, I scanned the other side of the street. Darkness filled the lanes of a drive-thru bank. My gun was out of the holster and cocked in less than three seconds.

Em shoved Jasmine into the back seat, telling her to lie down before screaming at me. *"Entra en la mierda del coche."*

Get in the car.

It went against my instinct to run. I was a fighter and a winner. I didn't walk away from a battle. Scanning the darkness in the direction I knew that the shots originated from, I aimed my gun. There was a flash or a reflec-

49

tion a millisecond before a bullet hit the car. I emptied a magazine, unsure what or if I hit someone.

"*Dame la llave*," Em yelled.

As I started to load another magazine, my gaze caught Jasmine, lying on the car floor in a fetal position. Her eyes were closed, dark makeup ran under her eyes, and she was trembling. Snowflakes still clung to her long hair, the white standing out against the red.

"Fuck." This might be a usual day for me and Em, but it wasn't for her.

I patted the key fob in my pocket before jumping in the front seat. My pistol was reloaded by the time Em started the car and hit the accelerator, driving us away from the battle I longed to finish.

Cursing in two languages, Em and I watched our mirrors and checked the side streets for more Russians. Once we were at least a quarter mile from the club, I turned. Jasmine was no longer on the floor. She looked as if she might be praying. Her face was buried in her hands on the seat, and her knees were on the floorboard. I reached for her shoulder. "Are you hurt?"

She shook her head and pulled away from my touch.

"Fuck." I laid my head back against the seat.

The capo would know about this. He might already know. That's what his soldiers were for, to update him on the happenings in his city. Probably before we returned, he'd get word of cartel and Russian gunshots.

I wiped my face with my hands and shot Em an oh-fuck glance.

"Jasmine, please talk to us," Em said.

"I'm fine." Her words were clipped as she moved to a

seated position, wiped her face with the back of her hand, and gasped for air.

Turning back, I looked at her in the strobing light from the overhead streetlights. Her complexion was pasty white.

"Stop the car," I said to Em. "Stop the car before we get on the highway."

"I'm already—"

"Fuck," I growled as I climbed between the front seats and over the console. It wasn't easy to get my long legs bent and my loafers through the space. Finally, I made my way to the back seat, lowered my tone and softened my timbre. "Jasmine, let me look at you."

She nodded, her lips pale.

I reached for her wrist. Beneath my fingertips, her pulse thumped rapidly. Looking in her blue eyes, I noticed her dilated pupils. Feigning calm, I smiled. "I need you to breathe for me."

"I'm breathing." Her words came out in gasps.

"Deep breaths." I sat tall and inhaled. "Come on. Do what I do."

"This is silly—" She looked past me to the rearview mirror.

Em spoke, "You could be in shock or going into shock."

Her hand went to her chest. "I can't get enough air."

I held both of her hands in mine. They were like holding ice cubes. "You can. Look at me." Slowly, her gaze met mine. "We're safe. You're safe. Now, deep breaths in..."

Jasmine complied.

In.

Out.

We breathed together as Em drove us back to the penthouse.

"You did great back there," Em said.

Jasmine blinked and exhaled. She retrieved her hands and pulled the zippered sweatshirt from the floor before putting it on. Once she had her arms in the sleeves, she rested her hands on her lap.

I, once again, took her hand in mine.

Her beautiful blue eyes slowly met mine. "I was scared."

"Good," I replied, "normal people should be scared."

"Were you?"

I shook my head. "We aren't normal, Jasmine. That's what we do."

She inhaled, her nostrils flaring. "One time" —she seemed to be on the verge of tears— "a man broke into my apartment. We think he roofied Piero."

I tightened my grip of her hand. "What happened?"

"He beat me up—wanted to scare me, but Piero woke, and he shot the man in the arm. We got away. That all came back to me at the sound of the shots."

More questions came to my mind—was she injured? Did he violate her? I knew now wasn't the time to ask her to relive either trauma. Pink was returning to her lips, and her hand was warmer than it had been minutes before.

I settled on the seat beside her and wrapped my arm around her shoulders, tugging her closer. It took a moment, but slowly, she began to relax. The tension eased from her muscles as she rested her face against my shoulder. "You're safe and the capo will probably kill Em and me on sight."

Jasmine lifted her head. "No, he won't."

My gaze met Em's in the rearview mirror. If we were smart, we'd take her home. Get her safely to the elevator. Ensure she's ascending to the penthouse and head straight to California. There were a few problems with that plan.

Number one, *mí padre* and *madre* are staying in the Ozarks, at the capo's mother's home.

Number two, I meant what I said when I told Jasmine I wanted to marry her.

Once again, Jasmine rested her head. "It's okay if you didn't mean it." Her voice was almost too soft to hear.

Reaching for her chin, I turned her face until I could see her gorgeous eyes. "Mean what?"

"What you said at the club. *El Patrón* will want his son to marry someone better than me."

"Marry?" Em questioned from the front seat.

She craned her neck, bringing her sapphire-blue eyes into view. "By Mafia standards, I'm now spoiled, having been out unsupervised with the two of you." She shrugged. "My sister wasn't interested in their traditions, but I can tell Dario respects them."

"That's bullshit," Em said. "We went for a drink. You weren't ravaged."

"No," she said, "just shot at."

My teeth were about to crack from the pressure.

"You're not spoiled," Em reiterated. "What the fuck about marriage?"

I repeated what I'd told Jasmine. *Mí padre* and the capo were in negotiations.

Em struck the steering wheel with his hand. "So is my father."

"*Mierda de toro*. That's not possible." My volume rose. "Andrés would need to go through *mí padre* first."

Jasmine sat up, pulling away from me. "Stop it. I'm not coming between friends. After all, you both saved me tonight."

For the next few minutes, silence prevailed. Not in my head. In my thoughts, I was challenging Em to a duel to the death. And then I remembered Herrera and the Russians. Our cartel didn't need infighting. We needed to be what the capo said: one family.

No longer resting her head on my shoulder, Jasmine sat pensively looking out the window. She wasn't currently an open book. Her expression was neutral in a way that would make the capo proud.

Em broke the silence. "We also got you into the mess."

Jasmine twisted her own hands in her lap. "Once Dario learns about tonight..."

She didn't finish her sentence, but we both knew upsetting the capo dei capi wasn't the way to win Jasmine's hand.

"The pass for the garage is in the console," I said as we approached the entrance to the capo's building.

As Em reached for it, Jasmine asked, "How did you get the pass?"

"Dante gave it to me."

She shook her head. "As soon as you scan that card, they'll know we're entering the garage."

"Maybe they've been too busy to notice we were gone," Em said hopefully.

I reached for my phone and turned it on to see eight missed calls. If that wasn't enough proof, the gathering of suited men near the elevator as we turned into the private garage let us know that they noticed.

"Fuck."

CHAPTER
SEVEN

Jasmine

Palpable dread filled the car as the crowd of men came into view. Tonight didn't go as any of us had planned, but that didn't mean that Rei and Em should suffer at the hands of the famiglia. The dark eyes of most of the men from our Christmas Eve dinner were staring our direction; however, there was only one set of eyes I sought.

I didn't wait for anyone to come forward to open the door. Instead, I bolted from the car in search of Dario. The sea of bodies parted until I was right in front of him, his arms crossed over his chest, pulling on the seams of his suit coat. I hadn't seen the expression he wore since the time I showed up at Emerald Club after my attack.

His eyes narrowed as he reached for my shoulders. "Are you hurt?"

Relief that he wasn't reprimanding me flooded my emotions. "No." Salty tears spilled from my eyes, yet I kept my voice strong. "I went with them willingly. They didn't do anything wrong."

By Dario's clenched jaw, darkening expression, and the way my heart raced, I knew that Reinaldo and Emiliano were both out of the car and standing behind me.

Dario released my shoulders. "Go upstairs. Wash your face. Later, we will talk."

Sniffing, I slowly turned, allowing the other faces to come into view. Dante, Jorge, Aléjandro, Salvatore, Carmine, as well as others from the cartel and guards from both sides. My heart fell as my gaze met Piero's. "I'm sorry."

"Jasmine."

I heard the female voice a second before Dario stepped aside, allowing me to see the open elevator with Catalina inside. She gestured for me to come to her. Instead of moving, I looked back up at Dario. "Please don't be upset with Reinaldo, Emiliano, or the cartel." I debated if I should say the rest, and I did. "They saved my life."

A murmur from the other men broke the looming silence of the underground garage.

With a flick of his chin, Dario wordlessly told me to go to Catalina.

Each step toward the elevator seemed more difficult than the last. It was as if I were walking through quicksand. I worried that it didn't matter what I said: Dario would do whatever he decided was best. Resisting the urge to take one last look at Reinaldo and Emiliano, I continued. Keeping my chin raised, I concentrated on Catalina's understanding expression, hoping I was reading it correctly.

She wrapped her arm around my shoulders as I crossed the threshold. It wasn't until the doors were fully closed that I gave into the emotion bubbling within me. Tears streamed as ragged sobs came from my chest. "What will he do to them?" I spoke into Catalina's shoulder as she embraced me.

"That's his decision."

Shaking my head, I looked up, meeting her green stare. "They didn't force me. I chose to go out with them."

She tilted her head. "Why would you do that? You know the dangers."

"I know the dangers." Stepping back, my words came out louder than I intended. I wiped my nose and cheeks on my sleeve. Exasperation overtook me. Lifting my arms, I let them fall to my sides. "I've spent my entire life surrounded by bodyguards. I thought for once it might be fun to live like other people."

Catalina pressed her lips together as the elevator stopped at the penthouse. "Dario would like you to go to your room and wait until he sends word."

"I'm twenty years old." The doors opened.

Catalina ran her palm over my arm. "I know, honey. I do. You're an adult, and you wanted to know what that felt like. However, now this situation is in Dario's hands. If I were you, I would do as he said. There's no sense in making the situation worse."

Make it worse—was that even possible?

What would Dario do?

I'd never encountered his wrath. Perhaps I'd been too afraid that he would send me back to the streets to disappoint him. Rei's threat of putting me over his knee came back to me. I knew that Dario was capable of bad things, but never had he even threatened corporal punishment.

We stepped into the foyer. My boots echoed on the marble floor. The living room that hours ago was filled with people was empty and dim. The only illumination came from the lights on the tree. Beyond the large windows, darkness reigned.

"Where is everyone?"

"Carmine and Salvatore sent their families home as soon as dinner was done. Anyone left who didn't go down to the garage is downstairs at Dante and Camila's apartment waiting for word about you."

"I'm sure Carmine used me as an example for how Isabella shouldn't behave."

Catalina pressed her lips together. "We can't know what goes on behind closed doors, but you are not an example of a problem. You're simply growing up. Isabella is only seventeen, I believe. She's not where you are."

My mind filled with the young girl with golden hair, striking for a young woman from an Italian family.

I went to the staircase and stared upward. Dario wanted me upstairs in my room like a child waiting for her sentence. A glance in the large mirror in the foyer told me why he said to wash my face. Mascara and eyeliner were smeared beneath my eyes. For some reason, I couldn't make myself climb the staircase.

Instead, I let out a breath and sat on the second step. "This is what it's like to have Dario upset with you."

Catalina sat beside me, tucking the skirt of her dress around her legs. "You know that if he didn't care, he wouldn't be upset." She laid her hand on my knee. "You said you thought it would be fun. Was it fun?"

"At first." I nodded, allowing myself to remember what had only recently happened. "Driving away without Piero or Armando was exhilarating. Have you ever wanted to do it?"

Pressing her lips together, Catalina shook her head. "I think I'm afflicted with an insufferable case of rule following. I have for my whole life."

Swallowing, I nodded. "I get that. I don't know about my whole life, but until tonight, I've followed the rules." A chill came to me as I thought about the first snow. A lump formed in the back of my throat as I willed away emotions. "Do you remember your childhood?"

Catalina inhaled. "Bits and pieces only. Nothing big. As a mother I want so much for Ariadna Gia as we can provide. I'm sure my parents wanted the same for me and my siblings."

"Birthday parties?" I asked.

She shook her head. "Not really. I remember my quinceañera. Do you have childhood memories?"

"I remember my eighth birthday." I wiped away a rogue tear. "Dario took Josie and me out to dinner." A smile formed, curling my lips. "I had a new dress and new shoes. We were all dressed up and the people at the restaurant treated me like I was a princess." My smile dimmed. "Before Dario, I don't really remember much, but Josie told me that before we got our own apartment, we'd stay with friends who would always end up kicking us out. For a long time, she worried Dario would do the same thing."

"No."

"I know he didn't..." I met her green gaze. "Do you think he will now? I'm old enough. He doesn't need to be obligated to me any longer."

Catalina's eyes opened wide. "Oh, honey, kicking you out isn't a possibility. He loves you." She tilted her head. "Do you want to be away from him?"

Inhaling, I tipped my head back and stared up at the ceiling. "Yes and no."

She smiled. "I remember thinking I was grown up enough to be on my own, but my father would never allow a female to live on her own. You have more freedom at college than I did. I commuted from home."

"I want freedom, but at the same time, I don't want to sleep in a car or be cold."

"That won't happen. You're Dario's family. That makes you part of our family. Right now, he's disappointed, and there's Salvatore and Carmine."

"They hate me."

"From what I've learned, they didn't care for Josie, and you're part of her. The fact you're a reason for a rift with the cartel...they'll try to take advantage of it."

"How?"

"Cause problems with the capos on the street. Make Dario look weak for not being able to handle you or soft for watching over you."

Cradling my head, I put my elbows on my knees and

closed my eyes. Each phrase she said was true. I never thought by leaving with Rei and Em I would make Dario look weak. I turned to Catalina. "It was just supposed to be a few hours."

"Where did you go?" she asked.

I met her gaze. "A place called Green Lady Lounge. It's a jazz club." I recalled the atmosphere. "It feels like you've walked into some old movie—red velvet walls and live music."

"I've never heard of it."

"I hadn't either. It's north off of 670."

Catalina's eyes grew wide. "What neighborhood?"

"I think it was around the Arts District." I scrunched my nose. "I'm not sure. It wasn't a great one."

She closed her eyes and exhaled. "Oh, Em." She shook her head. "They should have known better."

The hum of the elevator moving reverberated through the foyer. Catalina squeezed my knee. "They're coming up. Please go upstairs."

We both stood. "Will you come with me?" I asked. "So much more happened, and I would like to talk to someone about it."

"Of course. I'll check on Ariadna—she's in her crib— and then I'll come to your room."

CHAPTER

EIGHT

Reinaldo

I gritted my teeth as Jasmine walked toward Cat. I recalled the sweetness of her lips, the ferocity of her kiss. She shared my hunger. Despite her uncertainty, her body responded to me. Jasmine was meant to be mine. I felt it deep within me. I willed her to turn around. No, this wasn't her fight. It was mine. She'd already said her piece, defending Em and me. Standing taller, I clenched my hands in front of me, showing that I wasn't going to pull out a weapon. I was ready to take whatever awaited me. I'd show everyone present that I deserved Jasmine's hand. This wasn't the way I had planned on the conversation going down, but it was too late to turn back.

The ring of men grew as others stepped out, encircling Em and me. Not only was the capo dei capi staring us down, but also *mí padre—el Patrón*—and Andrés Ruiz, Em's father. My brother, Jano, met my gaze. He had my back, I knew that. I also knew that this situation put everyone in a difficult position. There were others watching and listening, cartel and famiglia alike. This was the face-off.

Together, Em and I had fought life-and-death battles. We were both still standing to talk about them. This wasn't our usual fight. We weren't getting out of this by using the weapons secured to our bodies.

As Jasmine disappeared into the elevator, I wondered if either of us would be allowed to see her again. The thought of not seeing her now that I'd told her about my intentions for her, was equally as unnerving as the stares we were receiving from all the men in attendance.

"We'll take this upstairs," the capo said, his dark stare burrowing into both of us.

I started to speak but stopped at the shaking of *mí padre's* head.

The capo continued, "This discussion won't be a spectator sport. Jorge, Andrés, and Dante will join us." He turned to his uncles. "While we're meeting, find out what you can about what happened over on Grand Boulevard." He turned to Dante. "Have you heard the final count?"

"Two of Myshkin's men are dead."

"Shot?" I asked.

"Rei, not your concern," *mí padre* reprimanded.

"Yes," Dante answered. "Myshkin's blaming us. Said we sent cartel soldiers to test our ceasefire."

Despite my father's reprimand, I spoke anyway. "You

didn't send me. However, I was the one who fired off a magazine. I didn't see the victims. It was too dark."

Dario turned his attention to me. "You? You took Jasmine to the Arts District at night?"

"Yes. We were ambushed—"

"With Jasmine?"

"Yes," Em spoke. "Our goal was to get her out of there once we realized Myshkin's men were present."

"Fuck." Dario shook his head as he shot a dark glance toward his brother. "We'll discuss it upstairs." He looked around. "Dante, communicate with the soldiers on the street. Everyone else, we'll see you in the morning for breakfast. Jasmine is safe and for now, so are Emiliano and Reinaldo. As for the fallout with Myshkin, we'll know more tomorrow." He turned to his guards. "Follow protocol for tonight. Your jobs haven't changed. Tomorrow we'll talk."

They nodded.

Piero narrowed his eyes at me.

Had he told what he'd seen last night?

Before stepping onto the elevator, Dante came forward. "I need your weapons."

"We're supposed to be one big family," I replied.

"We are," *mí padre* said. "Do as Mr. Luciano asked. You'll get them back."

Reluctantly, Em and I handed our guns and knives to one of the famiglia's guards. No one spoke as the elevator whisked our *padre*, the capo, Dante, Andrés, and us to the penthouse. The doors opened to the familiar foyer. Unlike earlier this evening, the penthouse was eerily quiet.

I glanced around, hoping to see Jasmine. Although I didn't see her, it was as if I could feel her presence and the aroma of her honeysuckle and jasmine scent. I glanced up the stairs as we headed into Dario's office, where we'd been earlier in the night when Aléjandro declared we would win the war.

Everyone remained silent as the capo took his time, taking off his suit jacket, loosening his tie, removing his diamond cuff links, and rolling up his sleeves. Finally, he took the seat behind his desk. The entire room held its collective breath.

His commanding voice filled the office. "If you had harmed Jasmine in any way, you would not be alive. Do you understand?"

"Yes," Em and I replied.

He stood, his hands splayed upon the top of his desk as he leaned forward. "Emiliano, you're my wife's brother. And you, Reinaldo, are Jorge's son. Because of that, your death wouldn't be assigned to a soldier. It would come directly from me." His nostrils flared and tendons pulled tight in his neck as he produced a long blade from a hidden holster and laid it on top of his desk. "My knife would have your blood." His volume rose. "Both of yours."

The capo sat, a vein in his neck visibly thumping.

"Dario," Jorge Roríguez said, taking a step forward. "If these two men were guilty of atrocities against your" —he hesitated— "daughter, I would condone their sentence. It sounds as if instead of monsters..." —he turned to us— "they were reckless, irresponsible, and perhaps impulsive. For that, I will be responsible for their punishment."

"You took her into enemy territory," the capo said.

"We didn't know," Em said.

"All my negotiations and you fucked it up."

Dante spoke up. "Make your case. Explain to my brother your intentions."

Inhaling, Em and I looked at one another.

Em spoke first. "Our intention was to have a little fun. Jasmine was never meant to be in danger."

"We wanted to break free from everyone for a little while."

"How did you end up in the Arts District?" Dario asked.

"Green Lady Lounge," I said. "It was open. Live music. The bratva men weren't planned. We weren't looking for them."

"That's their territory," Dante said. "One of the few areas on this side of the river where we cohabitate. The new relationship is strained. Killing two of their men on Christmas Eve could fuck up our arrangement."

"Then they fucking shouldn't have started by shooting at us," I said.

The capo lifted his hand. "They shot first?"

"Yes," we said together.

"There are bullet holes in the rear of the rental car," I went on. "Once Em saw them in the lounge, we immediately left to ensure that nothing would go down with Jasmine present. On the street, we were fired at. Em got Jasmine in the car, and I emptied a magazine into the dark toward the direction the shots came from."

The capo leaned back against his chair and turned to *mí padre*. "I trust you to make sure this never happens again?"

El Patrón nodded.

"Our alliance," the capo said, standing, "is still strong. We need to be on the same side to bring down Herrera. I will talk to Myshkin."

Papá came forward and the two men shook hands.

There was a sigh of relief until I said what was at the forefront in my mind. "Capo and *Papá*, this is probably the worst time, but as for my intentions with Jasmine..." They were both looking at me in a way that would have shut down a levelheaded, thinking soldier. "I want to marry her."

"Jasmine is not available to be wed," the capo said.

"Shouldn't that be her decision?" I looked to Dante for help.

Dante spoke, "Jasmine is in school."

"Camila is reenrolled," I countered. "Jasmine is an adult, and it's time for her to leave the nest. She should leave with me."

"Fuck," the capo said, looking around. "I wasn't planning on this conversation tonight. Jorge and Andrés have each mentioned the possibility that you both have interest. She won't wed either of you." He lifted his brows. "I'm in negotiations with someone else."

"What the fuck?" I asked, determined to not allow that to happen.

"She's not a Luciano."

"We know that too," I said. "Who? Who are you negotiating with?"

"If you were paying attention, you'd know the answer. Since you haven't been, I don't need to answer to you, boy."

Boy?

"Rei, that's enough," *mí padre* said.

"We have an alliance in place," I said. "Respectfully, her current last name isn't as important to me as her future last name." I took a step forward. "Sir, you know Jasmine's worth. It's why you keep her so very well protected." I brought my right fist to my chest. "I will do the same. With me, she will be my queen."

The capo pressed his lips together. "This will not be mentioned again during the holidays. You're welcome to remain in my city and my home through tomorrow. Stay away from Jasmine. My wife has plans for the holiday, and we will indulge her. Our minds need to be on winning our war. Is everyone agreed?"

CHAPTER
NINE

Jasmine

After scrubbing my face, I dropped the washcloth, cupped my hands and splashed water to remove the soap. Opening my eyes, I saw that my flesh was pink. Still, dark circles remained. I dabbed makeup remover on a cotton ball and wiped away the remaining mascara and eyeliner as my mind replayed the evening. If only I'd said no. If only I'd done what I usually did and followed the rules.

If I were honest with myself, I wanted another kiss. The one Em and I shared last night had run repeatedly through my mind. Never in my life had I been kissed like that. That wasn't true any longer.

Staring in the mirror, I ran my fingertip over my lips and sighed.

Rei's kiss in the booth.

Just thinking about it did something to my insides.

While Em's kiss set a high bar, Rei's kiss pole-vaulted over that bar. There was nothing tentative about Rei. What had he said last night in the living room? He'd said danger excited and turned me on. That was what it was like to kiss him, dangerous, exciting, and sexually awakening.

And to think the kiss I'd wanted was another from Em.

When he whispered in my ear and asked if I was ready to get out of here, I didn't consider the consequences. It was as much my body that wanted to go as my mind, probably more so.

The boots, jeans, and sparkly top were gone and replaced with pajamas by the time Catalina knocked on my bedroom door. "Come in."

The door opened, and to my surprise, my visitor wasn't Catalina.

Contessa's red and puffy eyes brought back my emotions. "Jasmine, child."

"I'm sorry."

"Are you hurt?" She came closer, reaching for my hands. "I was so worried. I've been praying." She scanned me up and down. "Did they...?"

From the first day we arrived in Dario's home, Contessa welcomed both my sister and me with open arms. More than a housekeeper or house manager, Contessa had been the grandparent I'd lost too early to remember.

I squeezed her hands. "No, I'm not hurt. I went with them willingly. We just wanted to have some fun and see the city without the normal restrictions."

Contessa took a step back. "You left willingly? With two dangerous men?"

"Aren't they all dangerous? Isn't Dario? Isn't Dante?" I spun in a slow circle, remembering Rei's comments about them being monsters. "Every man down there tonight at dinner is a killer. It's what they do."

"Not the same," she said. "The famiglia has honor."

My head tilted. "I've never heard you say anything bad against anyone before."

"Jasmine, you've been sheltered. There's a side of life you don't know about. Horrible things can happen to a young woman like yourself. Monsters lurk behind hand-some faces."

But were all monsters bad?

Contessa continued. "Josie wanted to protect you. We've all helped to do that, but one day you'll need to grow up. Not all men are the same as Mr. Luciano or Dante. Those young men. I see the way they look at you. You're not safe with them."

My neck stiffened with each of her words as a need to defend Reinaldo and Emiliano surfaced. "You are wrong about them."

"If Josie were here—"

"If she were here," I interrupted, "she'd want me to be happy."

"If she were here" —she paused— "a lot of things would be different."

Dario wouldn't be capo. The alliance never would have happened. Catalina would be only one of the cartel, not in our lives. None of them would be present. I missed my sister. That didn't mean I wasn't happy with the family we'd created.

"You know what Josie taught me?" I didn't wait for an answer. "She taught me to see the good in people. She could always find a reason to be hopeful. She also showed me what it's like to live a life that others don't think you're good enough to live. I would never think less of the men I've met from the cartel just because we have different backgrounds."

Contessa inhaled. "I'm not saying—"

"You are and that disappoints me. You can welcome Catalina and Camila but not the men in their family?"

"I worry for you."

My door opened and Catalina stepped in. "I'm sorry. Ariadna was awake. It took longer than I planned to help her settle."

"Do you need me to check on her?" Contessa asked.

Catalina smiled. "No, she's sleeping now. I think the company has her off schedule." She looked at me. "I can leave."

"Please don't."

Catalina nodded, closing the door and stepping inside my room. "Am I interrupting?"

Contessa reached for my hand. "I just want you to be safe."

"I am." I swallowed. "I love you."

Fresh tears formed in Contessa's eyes. "I love you. You're right about what you said. Even old women can learn to do better." She walked toward the door. "I'll let the two of you talk."

Once Contessa was gone, I sat on the floor, crossing my legs. "Will Dario come talk to me after he's done downstairs?"

Catalina shrugged as she sat on the edge of my bed. "I don't know. I'm not sure how long he'll be down there."

"Reinaldo and Emiliano stayed up here last night."

"They did. This place has too many bedrooms. Besides, it seemed weird to have Rei stay with Dante and Camila."

Yeah, he was supposed to marry her. I didn't mention that. Instead, I asked one of the questions on my mind. "Will Dario let them stay?"

"Em is my brother. Dario won't kick him out. To kick out Reinaldo would be an insult to *el Patrón*. Of course, Rei could go stay at the mansion with his parents."

"I'm sure Mrs. Luciano would love that."

Catalina scoffed. "Arianna has more bedrooms than we do. And she has the space to house the Roríguez soldiers." She looked down at her hands and back up. "I'm sorry to pry, but as I was nearing your room, I heard your voice...were you angry with Contessa?" She tilted her head. "And I heard your sister's name."

Exhaling, I sat back against my outstretched arms. "Contessa thinks I've been sheltered. It was what Josie wanted."

"It makes sense from what little I know about your sister's history."

I sat forward. "I'm sorry if it bothers you to hear Josie's name."

She shook her head. "It doesn't. You loved her. Dario

loved her. Her memory shouldn't disappear just because I'm here."

"I know Josie's history and mine, but I can't remember life before Dario and Contessa. I probably am sheltered. No, I definitely am. That was what I wanted to do tonight, have a chance to see life the way others see it."

"Contessa thought you were wrong to trust Rei and Em because they're cartel."

There was no reason to lie to Catalina. "She said I don't understand what horrible things could have happened to me. The thing is, I do. I'm sheltered but not naïve. I know why I have bodyguards. I trusted Rei and Em, and they didn't betray that trust."

She inhaled and exhaled. "I'm happy to hear that."

"They said something else."

"What did they say?"

"Reinaldo said he wants to ask for me. Marriage."

Catalina didn't act surprised. "What did you say?"

"Well, there's more. It seems they both are interested."

Catalina sat taller. "Dario will not approve of that."

I shook my head. "I don't think they were talking about sharing, more that one would choose me."

"If you could choose, who would it be?"

Lifting my hands to my face, I sighed. "That's the thing. I've been protected by being under Dario's supervision, but I also lost the ability to choose. If I wed, the groom will be Dario's choice. And after tonight, it may not be either one of them."

"He's an open-minded man, Dario is. He would take your opinion into consideration."

Before I could respond, there was a knock on my door. My eyes widened. "Speak of the devil." I stood and walked to the door.

Dario scanned my washed face approvingly before taking a step inside. "There's no way to sugarcoat this, Jasmine. I'm disappointed in your judgment."

"They didn't do anything wrong."

"Taking you away without consulting anyone. You lied to Piero."

"I told him I was going up to my room. I did."

Dario inhaled and exhaled. "Pack your things. Tomorrow after Christmas breakfast, you're headed back to Barnard."

"Dario?" Catalina questioned.

I spun toward Catalina, who was now standing. "He's kicking me out." I reached for my own hand, realizing it was trembling.

"No," Dario said.

Slowly, I turned back to him, unable to form words.

"Jasmine." His voice was less harsh. "This is your home and will always be your home. After we discussed things with Reinaldo and Emiliano, Dante and I received reports from a few of our capos on the street."

He was kicking me out.

Anything else he said was just noise.

Josie's fear had happened.

"One time," I said. "I disobeyed you once and you're done with me?"

Catalina came up and wrapped her arm around my

shoulders. "Let's listen to him. He said this is your home. It always will be."

I nodded, blinking away the tears.

"Reinaldo killed two men tonight."

"What?"

Dario nodded. "Myshkin is the head of the bratva in Kansas City and St. Louis. He has his soldiers on a mission to find the two cartel members and the redheaded woman with them. Jasmine, sending you back to Barnard early is for your protection."

"Aren't I safe here?"

"You're safer away from here for the time being." Dario turned toward the door.

"What about Reinaldo and Emiliano?" I asked.

He didn't turn. "They'll fight our war. That's what matters now." He walked away.

TEN

Jasmine

My heart raced as I woke from a troubled sleep, speeding from dreamland into confusion. A sense of panic rose up within me. Scanning my dark bedroom, I pulled my blanket over my breasts and searched the corners, certain I wasn't alone.

What is happening?

Is our home under attack?

A large figure moved from the shadows a millisecond before a hand covered my mouth, stopping my scream. The scent of alcohol filled the air as warm breath bathed my ear.

"Don't be scared."

The familiar deep voice resonated through me as I shook my head. I wasn't scared—alarmed and caught off guard. My pulse sprinted, causing my heart to thump against my breastbone. The reverberating beat in my ears made it difficult to hear Rei's question.

"Will you be quiet?"

I nodded as my nostrils flared. As soon as he released my lips, I gasped for air. "Reinaldo?" I whispered as I jumped back. "You can't be in here. Oh my God. Dario will definitely kill you." I wished that I was speaking metaphorically, but I wasn't. "Did anyone see you?"

"No one saw." The mattress dipped as he sat on the edge of my bed. His usual sandalwood-and-leather scent combined with alcohol emanated around us as he reached for my hand.

Cautiously, I let him have it.

He wrapped his fingers around mine. "If he finds me, he can try. *Mí padre* is sending Em and me back to California in the morning, early before others wake."

"On Christmas Day?" The sensation of his touch caused my skin to warm, and my eyes adjusted to the darkness, bringing Reinaldo's handsome face out of the shadows. The muscles in his cheeks tightened, revealing the chiseled edge of his jaw.

"I couldn't leave without talking to you."

I sat up, allowing the blanket to pool around my waist. My pajama top covered me, although my lack of a bra felt a bit scandalous. "I wanted to talk to you too. Was Dario too hard on you and Em?"

Reinaldo scoffed. "Not as hard as *mí padre*."

"He said you killed Russians tonight?"

"*Sí.*" Lifting my hand, he kissed my knuckles. "They want to keep us apart, but I had to tell you that I'm not wrong about you. You're deserving, more deserving than to marry a soldier—just a soldier. That's all that Em is or will be. He can't offer you what I can. I'm the second son of the kingpin."

"You know it won't be my choice."

He exhaled, as if nonverbally agreeing. My future was in Dario's hands.

"There was another reason I risked coming to see you." His hand cupped my cheek. "I want to kiss you again."

Hearing those words coming from him made my core twist and clench. "I want that too, but I don't think we should."

The tips of his lips curled upward. "I was right about you. You're a rule follower."

I momentarily lifted my hands to my face. My words came out muffled. "Until tonight."

Gently, he eased my hands away from my face. His dark orbs zeroed in on me as if he could see beyond my exterior before teasing a ringlet of my hair through his fingers. "I don't want to go back to California. I want to ensure you're safe." He paused. "Your beauty is also a curse."

"I don't understand."

"Em and I should have taken more time to learn more about where we were taking you. Fuck. We had no idea that the lounge was in Myshkin's territory. Jano told me that the Russians sent word on the street that they're looking for the beautiful redhead who was seen with two cartel members."

"Dario told me." A smile curled my lips. "He didn't add the *beautiful* descriptor."

"He should, *preciosa*. Like I said, you stand out among the others."

Preciosa?

My smile faded. "Dario is sending me back to New York tomorrow after breakfast."

"He's probably right, but I'd rather have you in Northern California with me." Rei bent at the waist and lowered his forehead to mine. "I fucked this up. I should have come forward sooner with my desires. Damn problems with Herrera."

He was so close. Even in the darkened room, I could see into his dark eyes. Reinaldo wasn't scary. He was intense, dangerous, and deadly. He was also risking his life to talk to me.

"It isn't your fault or Em's. I went with you willingly. I wanted to see the world without bodyguards for once."

The timbre of his voice lowered. "Is that the only reason you went with us?"

A wave of warmth flowed from my chest upward to my neck and my cheeks. I pulled away to see more than his eyes. My breathing quickened, causing my breasts to rise and fall. The focus of my gaze dipped down to his lips—his strong, firm, yet also tender lips.

Rei lifted my chin. His timbre slowed. "When you're mine, I can kiss you whenever I want." He ran his warm palm over my arm. "And touch you. It won't matter where we are, I'll take what is mine."

He said that as if it were already proclaimed.

"Without my permission?"

"No." He shook his head. "You will want it all. You'll crave me as much as I crave you."

My breathing grew shallower.

"My cock is so hard right now, I'm not certain I can walk away. If we could find a priest tonight, I'd show you exactly what I mean. Soon, you'll be as addicted to me as I am to you."

I rolled my lower lip between my teeth. "I went with you tonight because I wanted to get to know you better." That was what he'd said in the lounge.

His hand moved from my chin to my cheek.

I closed my eyes, savoring the gentleness in his touch. It was as if he were holding back the dangerous side of himself, wanting me to recognize that he could also be tender.

Lifting my chin, I brought my lips to his. Explosions like fireworks on the Fourth of July detonated within me as he moved his hand to the back of my neck, pulling me toward him. Our heads turned and noses bumped. There wasn't anything gentle in his kiss. Rei was ravenous and I was his meal. I also wasn't meek in this new dynamic.

He'd said I'd want his kisses and his touches. In a matter of three encounters, he'd proved himself right. I pressed back. It was as his tongue sought entrance that I pulled away.

"Rei, I can't...we're not married."

He shook his head. "I didn't believe there were women like you left in this world." He stroked my cheek with his finger. "The capo will choose me, and we will be married." He leaned closer, his black orbs focused on my lips.

My approval came in the form of a nod, a small, almost imperceptible, nod, but a nod nonetheless.

Our mouths collided again as a moan escaped my lips. Rei's tongue teased until my lips parted. He tasted of alcohol and danger, an absolutely intoxicating combination. I reached for his neck, wanting to touch his shoulders, pull him closer, and to feel his hardness against my softness.

This passion was the thing of movies and books.

I'd doubted its existence in reality, and yet here it was.

Rei's hands began to roam when he was the one to pull away. "Fuck, Jasmine, I want to fuck you, but I won't give the capo reason to hate me. The next time we're together will be our wedding."

My mind was too mushy to comprehend what he promised.

"Tell me you want the same thing."

I nodded, still a bit drunk on the endorphins speeding through my circulation. "I do."

"Then it will happen."

As he stood from the bed, I made a point not to look for proof of what he'd said about an erection. Instead, I kept my gaze on his eyes. "Rei?"

He reached for my hand. "I'll be thinking of all the ways to bring you pleasure once we're wed."

"What if Dario doesn't agree?"

"He will."

"How can you be so confident?"

A smirk came to his talented lips. "Because you're now mine. If Dario chooses anyone else, you'll be a widow before he has a chance to fuck you."

That wasn't the answer I was expecting.

"What about Em?" I asked.

"He can find his own woman. I've found mine."

Once again, he kissed my knuckles. "*Preciosa.*"

"What does that mean?"

"It means beyond beautiful—precious."

"Rei," I said, "please don't get caught leaving my room. Dario and Catalina are the double doors beyond mine."

"See, Jasmine. He knows your value. It's why he keeps you close." He leaned over and laid a kiss on the top of my head. "No kissing anyone else. You're mine."

"I'm yours."

"Dream of me."

I held my breath as Rei went to the door. He stood silently for a minute before opening it and disappearing into the hallway.

Settling against the pillow, I contemplated my choice. I'd agreed. I said I was his.

I recalled something he'd said. He was going off to war.

Now that I'd committed my heart, I said a plea, wishing Rei to stay safe.

CHAPTER
ELEVEN

Jasmine
Three months later

With the late March chill, I was still wearing my winter coat as I paced the foyer of the penthouse, waiting for Dario. This was the first time I'd been home since Christmas, and the lack of information was eating at me. Catalina had tried to keep me up-to-date on what she knew about the declared war, or most of it, but that wasn't much. Despite multiple text messages to both Rei and Em, none had been returned.

My spring break was last week, yet I was ordered home now. Piero and I flew commercially, and we're now back in Kansas City.

"Oh, you're home," Contessa said, coming from upstairs. "I have your room ready."

"Contessa, what's happening? Have you heard anything about Reinaldo or Emiliano?"

"No. I haven't asked. Mr. Luciano has been very busy. I'm sure he'll tell you what you need to know." She patted my hand. "When you're finished with Mr. Luciano, come to the kitchen. I made carfogn with strawberry jam, your favorite."

Feigning a smile, I nodded, one thing she said repeating in my mind.

What I need to know.

Being back in the penthouse didn't give me the same joy it once had. If anything, it felt confining as if my skin were too tight.

"Jasmine," Armando said, "Mr. Luciano is ready to see you now."

The last time I saw Dario, he told me to leave.

Lifting my chin, I walked toward his open office door. I nodded at the guard standing at the door before entering. Once I was inside, the door closed. Dario looked up from his desk. It took him a second as if he were trying to recall why I was here or even who I was, but finally, he stood, a bit of a smile coming to his face.

He hadn't changed, if anything, maybe he was a bit grayer. His appearance was as impeccable as it had been the first time we'd met. "Jasmine." He came around the desk. "Why do you still have your coat on? You're home."

I pushed my hands deep into the pockets of the long wool coat. "I guess I'm cold. Why did you call me back? I still have over a month of classes—"

Dario inhaled, his expression stopping my question.

"You didn't return for your spring break."

Swallowing, I stood taller, unwilling to admit that I didn't feel welcome.

Dario continued. "There's been a development that I needed to speak to you about—in person."

Reinaldo.

This was about Reinaldo.

My stomach twisted as I grew warm. Taking off my coat, I folded it and laid it over a chair. It didn't make sense for my hands to tremble, but they were. I'd been expecting this discussion. Over the last few months, I'd convinced myself that I was ready to be wed. Now that I was facing the reality, I was less sure.

And then another thought came to me. "The war. Has Reinaldo or Emiliano been hurt?"

Dario gestured toward one of the chairs in front of his desk while sitting in the other. "No. This isn't about them."

I sat, holding my own hand on my lap to keep it from visibly shaking. "I thought you called me back about marriage."

He inhaled, his nostrils flaring. "Have you been in contact with either man?"

I shook my head. "I sent text messages, but they haven't been returned."

"I could let you think that they didn't want to respond to you, but that's not fair."

Exhaling, I let out a breath. That was what I'd thought. "Why haven't they responded? You said they weren't hurt."

"Jasmine, I had to work out some negotiations. Having you communicate with either man would have only provided false hope."

"What?" I asked. "I don't understand."

"I had them blocked from your phone. Your text messages never went out. Things have escalated in Mexico, and I need every soldier from the famiglia and cartel with their minds on our war. Neither Reinaldo nor Emiliano needs a distraction."

Crossing my arms over my chest, I nodded. "Then why am I here?"

"Zhdan Myshkin."

Lowering my arms, I stared. "I don't know who that is."

"He's the son of the leader of the Kansas City Bratva, Kostya Myshkin."

"I thought you were at war with the bratva. What does he have to do with me?"

"Kostya has agreed to help us with Herrera in exchange for you wedding his son."

My stomach sank as if the floor had just been knocked out from below me. "Dario, I don't know this Zhdan. I can't marry him."

"You can. Catalina didn't know me. I didn't know her. Aléjandro and Mia had only met once. You will be meeting Zhdan this coming weekend. He'll be here to formally propose." Dario stood. "The ill will between the famiglia and the Myshkin bratva began with my father. This is our chance to stand together as we have with the cartel."

Fighting back tears, I stared at the man I always

thought would protect me. Standing, I slapped my hands to my thighs. "You're sending me away to the bratva? I disobeyed you once, and you're sending me away."

"Jasmine, sit down."

My nostrils flared as I fought to breathe. Instead of sitting, I turned a full circle, taking in his office, the big desk, the bookcases, and the windows. "You said this would always be my home."

"It is. Your escapade on Christmas Eve brought a few things to light. I'd wanted to wait until after you graduated college for you to marry, but the rest of your education will now be up to your husband."

"I want to marry Rei."

"Rei lost his chance when he and Emiliano took you away without permission. Zhdan is older and will keep you safe. We've identified another danger and reason to join forces with Myshkin."

"Older? How much older?"

"He's thirty-two."

"Rei is only twenty-five."

"Jasmine, stop talking about Reinaldo. Your future is set with Zhdan. We've identified another reason for you to marry sooner rather than later."

My temples pounded as I applied more pressure to my teeth. "Sooner?"

Dario nodded. "Your mother, Leah Renner, has been released on parole. You don't need to know much about her, other than she's bad news. If she finds out where you've been and who you've been living with for the last thirteen years, she will try to exploit you. Having the famiglia and the bratva behind you will make that impossible."

My mother.

"She's never tried to contact me. What makes you think she will now?"

"Our soldiers learned that after your appearance at the Green Lady Lounge, your identity was confirmed. Zhdan was at the lounge. His father had already brought up the idea of you wedding Zhdan. Once his son saw you, he became determined."

"Saw me." I shook my head. "There were a lot of people there."

"Your mother has a way of finding the wrong crowd. When she learns that I'm your guardian and Zhdan Myshkin wants to marry you, she'll see dollar signs. You're no longer a child. I could handle this my way, but it seemed like you should know what's happening."

"Your way...is..." I stood, meeting his gaze. "What?"

"Eliminate the issue."

I nibbled on my top lip. "Eliminate—kill? Maybe my mother wants to know me."

Dario pressed his lips together. "The alliance with the cartel has worked. Your marriage will broaden our alliance to include the bratva. Your mother exploited your sister for money and drugs. A leopard doesn't change its spots."

"Do you have proof that she's out?"

Dario walked around to the other side of his desk. Shuffling through some papers, he pulled out a gallon-sized plastic bag with pictures inside. "Are you sure you want to see these?"

No longer trembling, I straightened my neck and nodded. "I'm not a child. I want to know what you know about her." I extended my hand.

Dario gave me the plastic bag. "Our men took these pictures a week ago."

Sitting, I opened the bag and pulled the photographs out. The first one was of a dark-haired woman sitting on a bar stool with a cigarette between her fingers. "That's my mother?" I tried to feel something for the woman in the picture, but there was nothing.

"That's Leah Renner."

"Where is she?"

"I thought you said you went to the Green Lady Lounge."

"I did, but the walls were red," I replied.

"This was taken downstairs."

I didn't go downstairs.

I flipped to the next picture. The same woman was talking to a blond man.

"Our soldiers have confirmed that she has been asking questions about you. We believe she's planning on pitting the bratva against me or vice versa. The news of our ceasefire and potential alliance isn't widely known, and it has some adversaries, people who don't want it to work. Whatever she's doing, it's a dangerous game she's playing."

"Can I help you somehow find out what's happening?" I asked cautiously.

"You're not being used as bait for any part of this war."

"It seems like you've already made me part of it, an offering to the enemy."

Muscles in the side of his face pulled taut. "That isn't what you are."

I stood. "Then let me decide who I marry."

"You're not getting caught up in whatever Leah Renner has planned. Zhdan saw you and wants you. That makes you valuable."

My heart pounded in my chest. "Am I?"

"Are you...what?"

"Valuable, in your eyes."

His nostrils flared as he walked back to the other side of the desk and sat in his big chair. Placing his forearms on the desk, he lifted his gaze to mine. "If you don't know the answer to that question, I've failed you and your sister."

Tears prickled my eyes.

I retook my seat. "You haven't failed. I just never really knew..."

"Then I failed." He inhaled. "For that, I'm sorry."

A miniscule bit of self-worth grew within me. I shook my head. "Please don't be sorry. I have known I was safe and cared for. It's that the famiglia—"

"I'm now the famiglia, Jasmine. The others don't matter. We've lost soldiers, so have the cartel and bratva. As I said, there are rogue soldiers who don't want the agreement here in Kansas City to work. Last week, that danger hit close to home. Antonio, my cousin's husband, was killed with a car bomb outside Emerald Club."

"And by me marrying Myshkin's son, that will somehow stop? What if you can't trust them? What happens to me?" I had an idea. "Is Catalina a distraction with these wars?"

"Yes and no. Having people we care about is a liability. Catalina knows to stay safe."

Rule follower.

"If I could decide for myself who I want to marry, I'd no longer be a distraction for you." When he didn't speak, I added, "I'd like my phone unblocked."

"You will marry Zhdan. Neither Reinaldo nor Emiliano is your concern."

My grip of the chair's arms intensified. "I want to at least talk to them."

"I've convinced Carmine that Isabella is of marrying age. She's a Luciano. Jorge is thinking over the proposal."

The small hairs on my arms rose to attention as his words shattered my fragile feeling of self-esteem. Unwilling to give into the tears burning my eyes, I kept my voice steady. "The answer you meant to give me earlier was that I'm *not* of worth or value, not enough for the cartel. You think you can substitute Isabella for me because of last names." I stood.

"You're not leaving the penthouse," he said.

Turning, I gave him my best smile. "We'll see."

TWELVE

Jasmine

As I made my way up to my room, bits and pieces of my conversation with Dario cycloned through my mind, obliterating anything else with hurricane-force speed.

I've been promised to the son of Dario's sworn enemy.

My phone was blocked—Rei and Em hadn't ignored me.

My mother was alive, out of prison, and looking for me.

Dario gave *el Patrón* another option for Rei to marry—a better option, a Luciano.

Isabella.

Disappearing into my bedroom, I shut the door, closed my eyes, and leaned against the barrier. A deep sigh came from my lips. No longer did I see the penthouse as a luxurious mansion in the sky. I saw it for what it truly was and what it made me.

It was a gilded cage, and I was a prisoner in my own home. That wasn't the way I used to see it, but the veil had been ripped away. By offering Isabella, he made it clear that I wasn't worthy.

When I opened my eyes, I saw that my suitcases had already been deposited on my bedroom floor. Scanning the room, I wondered how different my life would have been if my mother had never been arrested or incarcerated.

What would life be like with her?

I was relatively certain she wouldn't make me marry someone I didn't even know.

Josie didn't like to talk about our mother, and my memories were nonexistent. Not knowing the details of one's own past created a void I didn't realize I'd hidden for most of my life. Curiosity spurred more questions than answers.

Why did Josie detest her so much?

What did our mother do to warrant the hatred of a person who taught me to see good in everyone?

I wasn't willing to take my new fate sitting down. Fighting Dario's decision alone was not possible. I needed help. Taking my phone from my purse. I went back to the first floor in search of the man who could help. I found Armando sitting at the tall library table in the front sitting room. With his jacket off and his holster showing, he was reading his tablet.

Armando looked up from the screen and smiled as I

crossed the threshold. "Jasmine." There was a welcoming tone to his deep timbre.

"Hey."

Armando was about fifteen years older than I, tall and muscular, even more so than Piero. He could be the poster child for the bodyguard persona. While Armando's current primary responsibility was Catalina's safety, he too had been present since our arrival and was an intricate part of my life. To some, I supposed that he would be intimidating, perhaps even frightening. That's not the man I knew. To me he was a gentle giant. "I need your help."

He turned off the tablet and sat taller. "Anything for you."

"Thanks." A grin curled my lips as I pulled my phone from my back pocket. "Dario informed me that there's a block on my phone, not allowing me to call, text, or to be called or texted by Reinaldo Roríguez and Emiliano Ruiz." I pushed the phone across the shiny table in his direction. "Can you please undo that for me?"

"Can I?" He nodded. "Will I?" He shook his head. "Not without Mr. Luciano's permission."

"Armando, please? If he didn't want me to get it changed, why did he tell me about it? Besides, shouldn't I have some say over something?"

"Let me talk to Mr. Luciano." He pushed my phone back. "From what I understand, neither of those men are part of your future."

"Friends. I want to talk to friends," I lied. The pain in my chest told me that they were both more important to me than simply friends. My feelings were strongest for

Rei. If I married Zhdan, they'd both be out of my life. I didn't like the thought of that.

"If he says it's all right, I'll be happy to do it for you."

Taking the phone, I murmured, "I guess that's better than a flat denial." Feigning a smile, I took the seat across the rectangular table from him. "We can wait for him together. I wouldn't want you to forget." I thought about my mother. "Did you know about my mother?"

His smile dimmed as he nodded. "What about her?"

I sighed. "First that she's out of prison. And second, I don't know anything about her."

"I learned about her when the two of you moved in. Mr. Luciano likes thorough research." His lips pressed together. "She's a bad seed. You don't want to have anything to do with her."

"Another subject that I have no control over."

"Jasmine." His voice softened. "You don't owe her anything. You don't remember, but mothering wasn't her thing. Whoring was. She raised you and Josie in the back room of a club not half as nice as Emerald Club."

"I don't remember that."

"It's why Mr. Luciano doesn't want you at Emerald Club. Also, the woman's a criminal. She killed a young man by selling him fentanyl-laced drugs—a college student."

"I'm just trying to get this straight. I shouldn't see her because she is a criminal—as in she did or does things to break the law, killed someone, and had sex for money?"

"Correct. I know Mr. Luciano made the decision to

tell you she is out of prison. If I were him, I wouldn't have darkened your life with the news."

I sat straighter. "Tell me how what she did is any different than what you do or Dario does?" I asked. "I don't think you've ever sold yourself to support your children, but I'm most certain the difference between my mom being a murderer and you or Dario is that to our knowledge, my mom has killed only one person. The famiglia owns Emerald Club. The club has prostitutes." My phrases grew louder. "Explain why she's bad, but you two and others aren't."

Armando lifted his hand and spoke softly. "I promised your sister to not tell you things that your mother did. I already broke that promise. I'll just say that you're right. We've never claimed to be good men. Those of us sworn to the famiglia do bad things for the right reasons. We have honor. In the case of Leah Renner, she sold drugs for drugs. Worrying about feeding her children was way down her priority list. Mr. Luciano doesn't tolerate illegal drug use."

I scoffed. "Come on, the famiglia and cartel sell it."

"Sells yes. Uses no." He leaned forward. "I doubt she's clean."

"Seventeen years in prison makes it hard to get drugs."

"The world isn't nearly as black and white as you believe it to be. There are shades of gray everywhere."

"What can you tell me about Zhdan Myshkin?"

It was as if a shadow passed over Armando's face. "Mr. Luciano has done his research."

"And..." I prompted.

"His father started Zhdan out as a brigadier. That's like our capos on the street. They oversee a group of boyeviks, or soldiers. Zhdan proved himself worthy. When the sovietnik, which is like our consigliere, died, Kostya made Zhdan his sovietnik. That means he works for and advises his father, the pakhan."

"He's high ranking."

Armando nodded.

"How does one become high ranked in the bratva?"

"Similar to the Mafia."

"He's in Dante's position," I said.

"Yes."

"Dario thinks less of the bratva than the cartel."

"Is that a question?" Armando asked.

"No. It's an observation. He'd marry me to the second-in-command of the bratva, but not to the third in the cartel."

Armando's expression softened. "I'm not sure why you think that, but it isn't true. Zhdan saw you at the Green Lady Lounge. He wants you."

I sighed. I thought Rei wanted me too.

After over a half hour, I peered out in the hallway. Dario's office door was still closed. "Do you have any idea when he'll be free?" I asked.

Armando shook his head.

Giving up, I made my way back upstairs. I had an idea. Taking my laptop out of my bookbag, I set out to learn how to unblock numbers on my cell phone. A few videos, and I had both men unblocked from my phone. What I didn't know was if I was blocked on theirs.

Only one way to find out.

I sent a text message to Rei. Before I began typing, I thought about all that was happening. Before I told him the news, I wanted to be sure he wasn't upset with me.

"Dario told me that he had your number blocked on my phone. If you get this text message, please text back. I promise I haven't been avoiding you since the last time we saw one another."

Sitting cross-legged on my bed, I checked my emails. There were a few follow-up correspondences with my professors. I'd emailed earlier this morning to tell them there was a family emergency back in Kansas City, and I didn't know how long I would be gone. All the professors who emailed back said that they would be happy to send assignments and tests for as long as I needed.

There were perks to smaller colleges. Also, being associated with one of the most powerful men in the country wasn't a disadvantage.

Letting out a long breath, I lay back on my pillows. My mind battled between Dario's announcement about Zhdan Myshkin and my mother.

What is she like?

What is he like?

What does she look like?

Is he kind?

He's in the bratva—kind probably didn't describe him.

What about Rei?

He's in the cartel, but he could be kind.

Did my mother want to give up custody or was she forced to?

The questions were never ending.

My phone lying next to me on the bed vibrated with an incoming call. My hands began to tremble when I read the name: Rei Roríguez. I'd done it. I'd unblocked my phone.

Was it too late?

"Hi," I said, fighting back tears.

"Fuck, Jasmine."

My lips curled at his pronunciation: *Jazz-mean.*

"I'm so sorry I haven't been in touch."

"*Preciosa*, I've been worried. Have you gotten my text messages? I was beginning to think you were blowing me off."

Warmth filled my cheeks at his concern and use of the endearment. I took the last part literally. "No to the text messages, and I've never done the other thing...but maybe someday."

Something sounding like a primal growl came through the phone. "When we're together, I'll let you read each and every one I wrote. I want to see your cheeks grow pink as you read the ways I want to make you feel good."

My cheeks were getting hotter imagining what they might say. "I'd like to read them. You can read the ones I sent as well." I thought about the warring cartels. "Are you safe?"

"*Sí*. As safe as we are in this world. We've lost good soldiers."

Em? I wanted to ask.

"Anyone I would know?" I tried.

"No, Emiliano is still alive."

"Dario told me" —my voice softened— "that he recommended another woman to Jorge for you."

"A girl, not a woman. And I told *mí papá* that it doesn't matter. My mind is set."

His words gave me some confidence. "Isabella is a Luciano."

"The only thing that matters to me is that you will be a Roríguez."

"He's promised me to someone else."

Rei's volume rose. "That's not possible."

Tears streamed down my cheeks. "He doesn't think I'm worthy of you."

"That's bullshit."

"There's something else you should know," I said with a tightening in my chest. "There's a reason I'm not good enough…" I let the words spill out. "When I was three years old, my biological mother was incarcerated. She was given a twenty-year sentence. All I know is that she's out of prison now and wants to see me."

"I didn't know she was out."

I sat taller and wiped my eyes. "You knew about her?"

"*Sí*. She doesn't matter. Your past isn't as important as our future."

"Does *el Patrón* know? If he does, he probably doesn't want you to marry—"

"He knows."

"I don't want to marry someone else."

"I told you what would happen if you did."

His words came back—*I'd be a widow before my marriage was consummated.*

Rei lowered his tone. "Tell me who the capo promised you to."

I could hardly get the name out between sobs. "Zhdan Myshkin."

"Myshkin? Fuck no."

"Rei, what can I do? Maybe if I could get to my mother."

"First, let me learn what I can about your mother. *Mí padre* will call the capo and put an end to the talk of you marrying a Russian. For now, stay with Piero and follow the capo's rules."

"I don't know if your father can change his mind. I'm tired of having rules."

"No, my rule follower. Soon, they will be *my* rules." There was something about that promise that twisted my insides.

The sound of other voices came through the speaker, voices speaking Spanish. I didn't want to end the call. "Is everything all right?"

"I must go, *preciosa*. Do not worry. We will be together."

Nodding, as more tears streamed down my face, I said, "I want that too."

Reinaldo

Ignoring the filth and debris on the street around our feet, I disconnected the call and turned to my brother, Aléjandro, second-in-command to our *padre*. "Fuck." I stuffed my phone in the pocket of my jeans to stop myself from throwing it.

"Qué pasó?"

"He promised her to a Russian." My fist connected with the metal dumpster, sending shooting pain up my arm. "Fuck," I screamed. The pain wasn't enough. Turning toward the brick wall, I balled my fingers into a fist and reared back.

Jano reached for my arm, holding back my punch. "*El alto.*" Forcibly turning me, Jano pushed me against the wall. "What the fuck?"

"The capo, he's promised Jasmine to a Russian—to Myshkin."

"No." My brother furrowed his forehead. "That's not right. He wouldn't do that."

"He's the reason I haven't been able to reach Jasmine. He put a block on her phone."

"Fuck, man..." He released me.

Cursing in two languages, I paced behind Wanderland, the cartel's club near San Diego. "I thought I'd scared her away with my text messages, but no. It was him."

Jano shook his head. "What the fuck were you texting her? You know the capo probably has access to all her text messages."

"Then it's a good thing he blocked me." Curling my lips was more of a grin than I'd had in a long time. "She wasn't blowing me off."

"And it sounds like she never will."

"He's wrong. I'm marrying Jasmine even if I have to go Dante-and-Camila on them."

Jano leaned back against the brick wall. "Don't do that. Fuck, I thought the house was going to fall and not by gunshots. Dante and Andrés about went to blows. I'm not sure the alliance can take another upheaval."

"The thought of anyone else touching her..." The pressure I applied to my molars was intense.

Jano laid his hand on my shoulder. "Use that anger down in the basement." He tilted his chin toward the back of the club. "They have Garcia."

I narrowed my eyes. "Garcia doesn't narrow it down. It would be like the famiglia saying they have Rossi."

"Manuel. Manuel Garcia. New kid to the crew. Has been working cleanup the last few weeks."

My time was supposed to be spent up north. I wasn't as familiar with the crews down in Southern California, and I couldn't stop thinking of some Russian with his hands on what is mine...

"Rei, focus," Jano said. "Manuel Garcia."

I shook my head. "Skinny kid, deadly accurate with a pistol?"

"Yeah, that's him. Nick discovered Garcia is a plant from Herrera."

"Well, fuck." We were losing soldiers left and right to Herrera. We didn't need to lose them to our own knives too. There'd be no other option if it's proven he's a traitor. "Is Nick positive?"

"Nick's taken over some of your web lurking for our region. He's good. Not as good as you, but he was able to triangulate cell signals and pick up text messages, even found deleted texts."

"Well, fuck. I guess you're right. I'll be talking to Jasmine instead of texting. If Nick can dig that deep, I'm sure the famiglia can as well."

"Focus, asshole," Jano said. "You and I are going down there. Nick and Em don't think he's the only spy. We need to learn what he knows."

Gathering information through torture was one of our favorite brotherly activities.

I gritted my teeth, seething with rage as we entered Wanderland through the back door. Looking around, I saw the crowd was sparse. Probably because it was still early in the day, only a few of the bars were open, and less than a fourth of the girls were present. "It's nice not having the whores around all the time."

Jano smiled. "That old school is working well as an apartment building. Mia has some great ideas. The whores like her."

"Is Mia going to keep working over there after the *bebé* is born?"

"We have over a month, but nonetheless, it's a point of contention. Liliana Ruiz is helping her. I'm not sure Liliana can take the lead. She's not much of a take-charge woman."

Opening the door to the basement, we were met with a hideous rotting odor. "Fuck," I said, lifting my hand to my nose. "Are they storing dead bodies down here?"

Jano shook his head with a shrug.

I reached for his arm. "Hey, before we start cutting off body parts, would you talk to *Papá* about Jasmine?"

"You realize the capo is my brother-in-law, right?"

"You're right. Talk to him. Tell him if he marries her to Myshkin, I'll kill the Russian and any thoughts of an alliance with the bratva are gone."

"Not interested in the younger Luciano cousin? Mia was shocked that Carmine would agree."

"Remember after Cat's wedding telling me that Jasmine was a scared little girl?"

Jano nodded.

"She isn't anymore. I haven't met Isabella, but Jesus, she's barely legal. Jasmine is the woman for me."

"I'll say something to *Papá*."

Four and a half hours later, I stripped down and cursed at myself for not changing shoes. These were thousand-dollar Italian leather loafers, and now they needed to be burned with the rest of the bloody clothes. After stuffing them all in a garbage bag, I stepped under the hot spray of the shower, in Nicolas's private office upstairs at Wanderland.

Blood combined with the water, leaving crimson-hued liquid swirling down the drain. I washed my hands for the fifth time—the damn rubber gloves broke at some point during the interrogation. The last thing I wanted was to have Garcia's blood under my fingernails. As I scrubbed my fingers raw, I concentrated on Jasmine. Hearing her crying ran on repeat in my mind. I wasn't even sure I heard Garcia's pleas for his life.

To my shock, the door to the bathroom opened.

"The fuck. I'm in here," I called beyond the foggy glass doors. Squinting my eyes, I saw a smaller person only a few feet away. My first instinct was to reach for my knife. I wasn't wearing a fucking knife in the shower.

Cursing under my breath, I looked around the shower stall for a weapon. There was shampoo, conditioner, bodywash, a cheap disposable razor, soap and the washcloth I'd brought in with me. The shampoo bottle was big, but not hard enough to do damage. That left me one option, my hands.

My thoughts filled with calculations.

I would need to distract the assassin.

With the shampoo bottle in one hand, I hurriedly opened the glass door and threw the bottle of shampoo. It narrowly missed the naked woman.

Naked woman?

"What the fuck?"

Long dark hair, made-up eyes with too much eyeshadow, and bright red lips were where I tried to concentrate my attention. The woman looked down at the bottle on the floor and shook her head. "*Hola,* Rei. I'm Julia. *Señor* Ruiz sent me up here to show his appreciation."

Wiping the water from my eyes and hair, I blinked before the realization of my nudity hit me. I reached for a towel and wrapped it around my waist.

Julia giggled. "Don't be shy. I didn't see anything to be shy about." She took a step toward me. "I promised *Señor* Ruiz to make you happy."

Fuck.

I never turned down a free fuck.

Never.

Stepping out of the stall, I reached for a second towel and handed it to Julia. "Wrap this around yourself, *por favor.* You can tell Nicolas that I'm not up for it today."

Her eyes widened. "If that wasn't up, I can't wait to see what is."

"Towel," I reminded her.

Reluctantly, she covered herself.

I shook my head. "Listen..." I've decided to commit to someone. I told her that I was her only one—only kisses, only touches, only pleasure. She deserved the same.

Okay, I didn't say all that.

"...I have a long drive back to Sacramento." I went to the vanity where my wallet lay beside my phone and key fob. Opening the wallet, I took out two one-hundred-dollar bills and handed them to her. "Take these."

Julia looked down at the bills and back up. Her lower lip was in a full pout. "*Señor* Ruiz will be upset."

"Don't tell him. Tell him that I fucked your mouth and blew a whole wad. You swallowed like a champ. My cock is still painted with your lipstick. I'll back up the story completely."

"You'll lie to the boss?"

A smirk curled my lips. "I wouldn't lie to the boss." *Mí padre.* "I'd lie to Nicolas Ruiz without an ounce of regret. If you get into any trouble over this, tell *Señora* Roríguez. She can get a message to me."

"*Señora*...Mia?"

"Okay, she goes by her first name. Yes, her."

Julia looked at the shower still running. "May I? It will be more believable if we're both wet."

Fuck, I could carry that conversation further. But I didn't want to. If instead of a thin and pretty Latina, I was standing nearly naked next to a beautiful, curved-in-all-the-right-places redhead, I'd definitely ask if she was indeed...wet.

I gestured toward the shower.

Julia dropped her towel to the floor and stepped behind the glass door. "Wait for a minute to leave." Her red-painted lips curled. "You would not come so fast."

Twenty minutes later, I walked out of Nicolas's office, a few minutes after Julia left ahead of me. Nicolas was waiting beyond the door with a shit-eating grin on his face. My words came forth in a primitive growl. "Don't ever fucking do that again."

"If you prefer redheads—"

Lifting my forearm to his neck, I pressed against his

throat, interrupting his words and pushing him back-ward. Our collective weight crashed into the wall. "If I were you, I'd think twice before you finish that sentence."

Nicolas's eyes bugged out before I released the pressure.

Coughing and reaching for his neck, he spat out, "*El Patrón* will hear—"

I pulled my blade from its sheath. The sight stopped Nicolas's sentence. "If you disrespect my future bride ever, it won't be my arm at your throat."

"You think you can threaten me?"

I shrugged as I put the blade back. "Seems like I just did. *Buenas noches*, Nicolas. I'll report to *mí padre* what happened tonight." With that, I turned and walked away.

CHAPTER

FOURTEEN

Jasmine

I'd done as Dario said and stayed in the penthouse. More specifically, I stayed in my room, hoping that Rei would call me back. Finally, I fell asleep. Contessa must have come in during the night or early morning as there was a tray of food when I woke. I hadn't been downstairs for dinner. There was nothing I wanted to say to Dario.

My eyes were puffy and sore. A shower and dressing did little to help my mood. There was one option for me. Technically, I was leaving the penthouse, but not by much.

Taking the elevator, I went down one level to Camila and Dante's apartment. Camila had been in a similar situation with her father promising her to Rei. I sought advice. "Hello," I called as the doors opened.

"Down here." Camila's voice, sounding distressed, came from the hallway to the right, the opposite direction from their living room and bedroom.

Panicked by possibilities, I hurried her direction. I came to a stop at the door to their workout room.

Wiping perspiration from her forehead, Camila grinned. Her feet were moving fast on the inclined treadmill. "I'm almost done," she panted. In front of her were large windows showcasing the dreary late-winter gray sky.

"You sounded like you were in pain or danger."

"I am," she said with a laugh. She tilted her chin toward a screen. "This program is full of hills, and I hate it."

I leaned against the doorjamb. "Then why do you do it?"

She continued to run. "I used to swim every day. After a few months of not exercising" —her cheeks pinkened— "not exercising without Dante because that can be a workout."

Pressing my lips together, I shook my head.

"I thought I was gaining weight."

Scanning Camila's frame as the treadmill started to slow, I doubted she was larger than a size four. In workout pants and a tank top, she was youthful and beautiful. If she was considered overweight, I needed to go on a strict diet. "You look fantastic."

She used her towel to wipe her face again. "Thanks." Camila inhaled. "What brings you back from school?" She did a double take in my direction and her smile faded. "Are you all right?"

"Dante didn't fill you in?"

"He's been working constantly especially since Antonio was killed. Antonio had been the one helping Dante run Emerald Club and now…"

I hadn't given that news any time in my brain. Now I recalled Dario mentioning that his cousin's husband was killed. "How is Giorgia?"

"Not well. Mia wanted to come back here for the funeral and to console Giorgia. Apparently, they were always close. Aléjandro won't allow her to travel with the baby due in a little over a month. And because Antonio and Giorgia never had children, the famiglia is making her move back in with Francesca."

"You mean Dario is making her."

Camila pressed her lips together and nodded. "Dante agrees. He says it's too dangerous with the threats from Herrera and until things settle with the bratva."

Settle—as in giving me to them as a sacrificial lamb.

Pushing that away, my thoughts went to Mia. She too was married and a childless widow before she was made to marry Aléjandro. "Dario won't make Giorgia remarry, will he?"

Camila shrugged.

"Gah," I called out, lifting my face to the ceiling. "I'm so over men making all the decisions. They say it's about safety. It's not. It's about control."

The treadmill beeped as the conveyor slowed to a stop. Camila held on to the railings and bent at the waist breathing deeply. "My legs are Jell-O." When she looked up, she was grinning. "I get it. Honestly, I hated it when it was Papá. I don't mind Dante having control."

"He's your husband. I don't have any control, and I don't have a husband or a father."

"You have Dario."

"Did Dante tell you that Dario convinced Carmine Luciano that Isabella is of marrying age?"

"No," she said, shocked. "Who does Dario want Isabella to marry?"

"Rei." My nostrils flared as I said his name, yet I managed to keep tears away.

"I can't believe Carmine agreed to that." Her eyebrows danced. "I guess that means you are available to marry Em."

My arms dropped to my side. "I like Em."

"But you like Rei more?"

"It's different. Rei makes my pulse race and my stomach twist. Em is sweet."

Camila laughed. "He's my brother, and he can be sweet. He's also a killer like the rest of them." Camila's mouth opened wide. "Wait. So, Dario took you out of the running for Rei?"

Dropping my chin, I replied, "Yes. He's tried." What little I'd eaten churned in my stomach. "He promised me to someone else."

"Shit." Camila's green eyes grew wide. "Not Rei or Em? Who?"

"Zhdan Myshkin, Kostya Myshkin's son."

She came closer and reached for my hands. "Dario wouldn't do that."

My tears were back. "He told me yesterday."

"We have to change his mind."

I met her green gaze. "How?"

Camila pouted her lips.

"I thought Rei wanted to marry me," I said. "And then I thought he didn't because he didn't respond to any of my text messages. I found out yesterday the reason why. Dario had both Rei's and Em's numbers blocked on my phone."

She extended her hand. "That I can help. Give me your phone. My *papá* did that to my phone whenever he thought he could control who I talked to. I know how to unblock them."

A grin lifted my cheeks. "I watched a few YouTube videos and figured it out."

"Did you get ahold of Rei or Em?"

"Rei," I replied. "I texted him last night, and he called me back."

Camila nodded. "No more texting. If Dario is having your phone watched, he'll see the text messages. Calls only. After you hang up, delete the call from your phone's call log. It's not foolproof, but it will make it harder for Dario to know."

"You're helping me communicate with Rei? Dario's your brother-in-law, twice over, and your capo. You're supposed to follow his rules."

She shook her head. "I bucked the system and got away with it. If you want Rei and he wants you..." She exhaled, sat on a big plastic ball, and widened her stance to balance. "It's great for the core."

"I've been thinking about Rei and marriage since last Christmas. When Dario called me to Kansas City, I thought he would tell me that my wedding date to Rei was set. At first, I was nervous. But when that wasn't the case, I was mad...and heartbroken. I don't know Zhdan Myshkin. I know nothing about the bratva. I don't want anything from Dario. No big wedding." I slapped my hands against my thighs. "I guess I want one thing. I want his blessing to marry Rei."

"Weddings are overrated," Camila said, standing. "Come to the kitchen with me. I need some water."

"Did it bother you not to have one—a big wedding?" I asked as we made our way down the hallway, past the elevator, and into the kitchen. Having a wedding like Dario and Catalina's was never a dream of mine.

"Honestly, not in the slightest. We had a priest and a license. Papá wanted to annul our marriage. Because it was blessed and legal, he finally saw the light." She opened the refrigerator and pulled out two water bottles. "Here."

I took the cool bottle and sat on a tall stool at their breakfast bar. "Do you think Rei and I could do the same?"

She shrugged. "How worried are you about Dario being upset?"

"I want to say not at all, but the truth is on a scale from zero to ten, I'm a nine."

Camila pressed her lips together and hummed. "What if you two wed in Mexico?"

"Why would we do that?"

"Because marriages in Mexico are recognized in the US." Her green eyes opened wide. "I have an idea but first tell me if this is what you want."

My heartbeat accelerated and my skin chilled. My mind told me that my physical reaction was because I was a rule follower. My heart knew what it wanted. "It's what I want."

I didn't need the permission of a parent. I was an adult. "Maybe, if I can't have Dario at my wedding, I could have another parent."

"Cat?"

Taking a drink of water, I shook my head. "No. My mother."

Camila sat at the seat by my side. "Your mother. I'm sorry. I assumed she had passed away."

"No, incarcerated." I'd never been able to say it with such ease. I turned to Camila. "She's out of prison. I haven't seen her in over seventeen years."

"Oh my gosh. That is amazing. Where is she?"

"I believe she's in Kansas City." She was in the pictures Dario showed me. "I don't know for sure."

"How did you find out?" Camila asked.

"Dario told me about her release and that she wanted to see me. That's the other reason he called me back to Kansas City. I want to go to the Arts District to ask about her, but I never learned to drive, and I can't ask Piero."

"I can drive. Dante would want me to take Giovanni. He could drive us." Her eyes widened. "Oh, we could have lunch at Taha Mexican Kitchen. I've been craving spicy food."

"I would love to get out of here, but there's a reason I was thinking of the Arts District." I exhaled. "Never mind, it doesn't matter. I don't think Giovanni will agree."

"Why?"

"Because the pictures Dario showed me of my mom were taken at the Green Lady Lounge, bratva territory."

Camila let out a long breath and sat back. "How is your mom connected to the bratva?"

I shrugged. "I don't know that she is. Dario said she's been asking questions. I was born in Kansas City. Before we moved in with Dario, Josie and I lived in South Blue Valley. I did a deep dive on Leah last night and accessed court records. She was imprisoned at WERDCC. That stands for the Women's Eastern Reception, Diagnostic and Correctional Center. It's in Vandalia, Missouri. Since she was convicted in Missouri, it makes sense that she was incarcerated here."

"Do you think she met people in the bratva in a women's prison?" Camila asked.

"I wonder a lot about her. I never did before, but now that I know she's close..."

Her lips opened in a gape. "Oh, the Green Lady Lounge. Isn't that where Rei and Em took you Christmas Eve?"

"I don't have any other ideas."

Camila scrunched her nose. "I want to help you, Jasmine, but I don't feel comfortable going into enemy territory, and I don't think you should either."

"I don't know why not. Dario wants me to marry Zhdan. I'd live in that territory."

Her emerald eyes lit up. "Have you tried calling instead of going there?"

"Why didn't I think of that?"

"Call the Green Lady Lounge and tell them you're looking for her. It's a long shot, but maybe you'll get a connection. Dante wouldn't want me to go into Myshkin's territory, but if you could speak to your mom, maybe you could meet her someplace safer." Camila hopped down from the tall stool and went to the kitchen table where her tablet was sitting. "Let's look up the number for the Green Lady Lounge." She began typing on the keyboard. Her smile returned as she brought the tablet to me. "You call and I'm going to message Mia. She helped me get married. She will help you."

"No, she won't." My hopes faded. "She's a Luciano. She hates me."

Camila pressed her lips into a straight line. "She's a Roríguez now. When I first met her, I wasn't impressed. Since marrying Jano, she's changed."

"Is there anyone else you can call? I don't feel confident about my marriage hopes depending on Mia Luciano."

"Roríguez. Let me try Mia." Camila walked into the living room with her phone.

I pulled my phone from my back pocket and called the number on the screen. It was only eleven o'clock. More than likely, the Green Lady Lounge wouldn't even be open. As I was about to hang up, I heard a voice.

"Green Lady Lounge, how can I help you?"

My hands began to tremble. "This is a long shot, but I'm looking for Leah Renner."

"No one works here by that name."

"I was wondering if you knew how I could get ahold of her."

"Why are you looking for Leah?"

"Do you know her?" I asked.

"Yeah, I know her, but I don't give out personal information without a reason."

"I'm her daughter."

FIFTEEN

Reinaldo

My home office was ostentatious and smothering just like the mansion where it was housed. This place belonged to Gerardo Ruiz, brother of Andrés and Nicolas. *Mí padre* put a lot of trust into the three brothers, all of them making it to the rank of senior lieutenant in the cartel.

Like many men their age, the Ruiz lieutenants had difficulty with Aléjandro's and my advancement in our father's organization. Case in point—Nicolas's ridiculous show of sending a whore to me while I was showering. The only one to support the alliance with the famiglia was Andrés. He had little choice. His two daughters, Catalina and Camila, were married to famiglia, Catalina to the capo dei capi himself.

Gerardo Ruiz's deception topped that of his brother

Nicolas. Unwilling to accept that Jano was his superior, Gerardo partnered with our enemy Elizondro Herrera in an effort to sabotage the Mafia alliance and bring down the Roríguez cartel.

That kind of treachery was not tolerated.

Gerardo Ruiz was no longer living.

Upon his death, *mí padre* sent me to Northern California to oversee our business in the region. This mansion belongs to the cartel, hidden behind numerous LLCs. That was why I was currently sitting behind a big-ass desk in a house ten thousand more square feet than any man needed, especially a bachelor.

I wasn't alone. There was plenty of space to house guards and household staff.

Jano and I grew up in a large mansion. I wasn't unaccustomed to luxury, but that didn't mean that I liked it. I meant what I said when I'd told Em I'd rather move back into his pool house. Jano and I lived there for a short time before Jano married Mia and bought his own mini mansion on a cliff.

I made a few revisions after a recent attack on the house and grounds. Nevertheless, it was too large.

My vision blurred with weariness as I completed reports, fulfilling my duties. I was ready to fly east, and I didn't give a fuck if I had any sleep before I did. I hadn't had any since talking to Jasmine and torturing the spy.

Between calls with soldiers in the area, I did what I do well. I researched Jasmine's mother and Zhdan Myshkin. I didn't expect the two searches to intersect. They did.

As I'd told Jasmine, I'd known about Leah Renner

ever since Jasmine was recommended to me. I had a standing internet search on her mother. For some reason, the search wasn't triggered with her release. The more I learned, the less I liked the idea of Jasmine making contact with her.

It wasn't only because her mother was a felon. If I or any other member of the cartel had an issue with people who broke laws, our circle would be entirely too small. Breaking laws and getting caught were two different things.

Leah Renner was caught.

The defense tried to play Leah off as an innocent victim of the Smirnov bratva, the predecessor to the Myshkin bratva. She was given the tainted cocaine and passed it on without knowledge of the fentanyl content. The judge nor jury cared where Leah Renner received the illegal drugs. The fact that she had multiple priors for drug use, child endangerment, and prostitution didn't help her case.

The parents of the dead college student had money, enough to help the wheels of justice put Leah away for the maximum penalty of twenty years at a women's prison in Vandalia, Missouri. Her early release on parole was due to prison overcrowding.

"What the fuck?" I said aloud as I read about multiple visits to her in prison by a man named Dmitri Makarova.

According to the records I accessed from the women's prison, he began visiting Leah around the time her case was scheduled to go before the parole board. Opening another screen, I researched the parole board. It took a few hoops, and I had more information.

While most people don't list their association to a Mafia family, cartel, or bratva on their LinkedIn resume, there were a few telltale signs. In California, Volkov Construction, Inc. was the cover for the Volkov bratva. In St. Louis and Kansas City, Smirnov Properties was the cover for the Myshkin bratva.

Dmitri Makarova was employed by Smirnov Properties.

Zhdan Myshkin, the man the capo wanted Jasmine to marry was his father's sovietnik, or counselor or advisor. Dmitri reported to Zhdan.

I looked at the clock in the corner of my computer screen. It was only a little after seven in the morning. That would be two hours later in Kansas City. I picked up my phone to tell Jasmine that no way in hell was she going to approach her mother, not without me at her side and an army at her back.

Maybe it was my lack of sleep, but the information I'd found heated my blood, filling my nervous system with alarm. Dmitri Makarova visited Leah Renner for one reason, and she was too dumb to realize that it was because Dario Luciano was her daughter's guardian.

"Fuck." Staring at my phone, my gut told me to call the capo directly. He didn't want to hear from me after Christmas Eve, but he needed to know that Jasmine was in danger. Going through my contacts, I came to the conclusion that I didn't have the capo's direct number. As I started to call Jano, my phone rang.

Mia's name was on the screen.

"*Hola*, I was about to call your husband."

"He's not home right now. Do you have a minute to talk?"

"I need your brother's number."

"Dario or Dante?" she asked.

"I have Dante's. I need the capo's."

"From what I've heard, he doesn't want to talk to you."

"Fuck him. He doesn't have to talk. He needs to listen."

Mia's voice lowered. "Rei, be careful. Dario didn't become capo dei capi by being lectured to."

"He's going to listen to what I have to say."

"Okay, I'll give you his number," Mia said. "Before I do, I promised to talk to you about Jasmine."

"Are you going to try to talk me out of marrying her?"

"I've made it my mission to advocate for consensual marriages. That means if she wants to marry you and you want to marry her, I'm on your side. Did you propose?"

I scoffed. "I told her she was mine and the next time I saw her we'd wed."

Mia made a noise. "You men are such pigs."

"But you love us."

"I love Jano. For the record, he proposed."

"After the capo informed you of the upcoming nuptials. The problem is the capo. He thinks he can marry her off to a Russian."

"That's what I heard. Did you know," Mia asked, "that marriages in Mexico are recognized in the United States?"

"You're suggesting that I kidnap Jasmine and take her out of the country?"

"No. But if you can get her, I know the perfect place for a wedding with your brother, pregnant sister-in-law, and parents."

Impossible. Jano wouldn't let Mia travel. And my parents…"My parents are out on Bella."

"Exactly, floating Mexico off the California coast."

"Fuck, Mia, you're a genius. Now how do I get Jasmine?"

"I can't think of everything. I also can't take full credit. It was Camila."

"Camila is in on helping me marry Jasmine?"

"We live in a strange world. Let me get you Dario's private number. You might not want to lead with your plans to kidnap his…whatever Jasmine is."

"My future wife is not to be disrespected."

It was as if I could hear my sister-in-law's smile. "That's what you need to show Jasmine and Dario, the irresistible Roríguez possessiveness. Some see it as charm."

A few minutes later, I heard the ring of my call to the capo dei capi. Another glance at the clock told me it was too early for a shot of tequila.

I hadn't slept. Didn't that make it still late?

"Dario here."

"Sir, this is Reinaldo Roríguez."

"I know your number, Reinaldo. Why are you calling?"

"I'm concerned about Jasmine."

His voice deepened. "She isn't your concern."

"She is and will be, but that's not why I'm calling you. I'm calling because I was informed that Leah Renner is out on parole."

"How would you know about her?"

"Did you know all you could about Cat before you married her?" I asked.

"I've learned more important things since then."

"I meant it when I said that I plan to marry Jasmine. I've done my research. *Mí padre* knows about Jasmine's mother and her sister. It was recently brought to my attention that Leah Renner was released. This morning, I started to do research—"

"Not your responsibility." His voice was firm. "The famiglia will take care of this."

I jumped to my feet and recited all that I knew before he could hang up on me. Mia might be right about the capo not wanting a lecture. That wasn't going to stop me. "Before her release, Leah was visited by a man named Dmitri Makarova. He works for Smirnov Properties. Makarova didn't begin to visit Leah in prison until she was scheduled to have her case reviewed by the parole board. Two members of the parole board received significant deposits of cash into their bank accounts after the board ruled to release Leah early. Both of those deposits were labeled as Jackpot.com. What are the chances that two members of the same board both won Missouri Lottery Prizes?"

"Will you send me that information? I'll admit, we didn't have that."

"I will." I continued my information dump.

"Makarova reports directly to Zhdan Myshkin. Someone—"

"How do you know about Myshkin?"

"Just listen. From what I can deduce, it appears that one or both of the Myshkins sent Makarova to the women's prison because Leah was of some value to them. They paid off the board to release her. Why would Leah be of value to the bratva?"

"When did Makarova begin visiting Ms. Renner?" the capo asked.

"October of last year."

"Fuck, that was the beginning of our negotiations."

"They want Jasmine to get to you. You can't allow her to be close to Zhdan. There's more to this than we can see. Jasmine will be collateral damage, and Myshkin doesn't give a damn. If what I learned about prior charges of child endangerment regarding prostitution and trafficking connected to Jasmine's sister are correct, Leah doesn't give a fuck either."

"How did you learn all this?" he asked.

"I'm fucking good at what I do. Capo, don't allow Jasmine to meet with Zhdan or her mother."

"She's not. She's here with us, where she's the safest."

"I'd like your permission to marry her."

He was quiet for a moment before speaking. "Jasmine isn't a fair offer for the alliance. Especially with what's happening with her mother."

Gripping the phone tighter, I paced behind my desk. Beyond the windows I stared at the lap pool and well-tended gardens, trying to find the right words. "If anyone is undeserving in our possible match, it's me. You're aware of Jasmine's value. If you weren't, you wouldn't be so protective of her."

"She's safe here."

"I'll send my findings to Dante's email and then I'm getting my bride."

"You have a job to do in California."

I took a deep breath. "I'll do it with Jasmine at my side. Myshkin won't be able to get to her here."

"I need to see what you found."

I leaned over my desk and hit a few keys. "Sent." I disconnected the call.

CHAPTER

SIXTEEN

Jasmine

Being in a restaurant felt like being let out of prison, and I owed it all to the coconspirator at my side. Her desire for spicy food had Camila and I sitting in one of the nicest Mexican restaurants in Kansas City. The bar in front of us was lined with the best of the best, top-shelf liquors. Our plates held varying degrees of spicy dishes. Even the aroma of Camila's enchilada made my eyes water. I opted for something less fiery. We also enjoyed chips and queso.

The margarita was a welcome surprise. Dario didn't mind if I drank wine in the security of the penthouse, but being only twenty, my drinking out in public was frowned upon. I wasn't certain how Camila did it. When the bartender asked for our IDs, she said something to him in Spanish. The next thing I realized, we were being

137

served. The large glass filled with frozen margarita brought a smile to my face and a scowl to our bodyguards' lips.

"It's not like either one of us is driving," Camila whispered.

Truly, after the last twenty-four hours, drowning in a margarita seemed like my best fate. It wasn't like I had many options with Giovanni and Piero standing patrol.

Camila took another sip of her margarita. "It's nice to get out of the apartment sometimes." She turned to me. "I hate when Dante works all the time. I get that he's busy. I'm glad I have my classes. Still" —she pouted— "I feel like I hardly see him." Placing her hand over mine, she smiled. "I'm glad you're home. I'd be bored without you."

"It is nice to get out of that prison." I reached for what was left of my margarita and swirled the ice. "I wish we could do it without our shadows." As I swiveled to look at Piero, I accidently bumped into the man to my right. Maybe if he wasn't so close... Turning, I saw the lightest blue eyes. "Excuse me."

His stern expression softened. "Excuse me."

My breathing caught and my heart rate increased at his Slavic accent. "Um, excuse me." I hurried down from my barstool and made my way down the long hallway to the bathroom. There was something familiar about the man, something I couldn't put my finger on. Whatever it was, the brief encounter had my heart racing. My reflection in the mirror was unusually pale.

The bathroom door swung open. "Are you all right,

Jasmine?" Camila rushed toward me and reached for my hands. "Your hands are freezing. What happened?"

Retrieving my hands, I went to the sink and turned on the hot water. "Probably from the margarita." Placing my fingers under the hot stream brought back the circulation with a painful prickling sensation.

"No. You look as if you've seen a ghost."

I turned off the water and faced Camila. "That man, the one who sat next to me at the bar." My stomach twisted. "Dario said that Zhdan saw me at the Green Lady Lounge. There's something about that man that seemed familiar—his blue eyes. His accent is Russian, I think."

"It can't be him. I mean, what are the chances?"

"I'm sure you're right. I just wish Rei would call me back or I could reach him. I missed his call when I was in the shower. I've tried to call back, and it goes straight to voicemail."

"Do you think Dario blocked your phone again?"

"I checked. That's not it. When he did that, I couldn't even reach voicemail." Wrapping my arms around my midsection, I inhaled. "I'm freaking out over nothing."

"You were told yesterday that you must marry someone you've never met. It's perfectly reasonable for you to imagine that every handsome Russian is your future husband."

Looking at Camila, I broke into a fit of laughter. "There's absolutely nothing reasonable about anything you just said."

She locked elbows with me. "True. But you laughed. Let's go have one more margarita before we head home."

"One more and I'll spend the afternoon asleep."

"Do you have better plans?"

"Sadly, no." I pulled the door open.

Camila and I stopped dead in our tracks. The man from the bar was there, blocking our exit. I stared at the buttons on his white shirt. Tipping my chin upward, I scanned his thick neck, defined jaw, and up to his blue eyes. Camila had called him handsome. The first time, I only noticed his eyes. My mouth went dry as I took in his becoming features, a negative copy of Rei. This man had blond hair and stunning blue eyes.

"Excuse us," Camila said.

His gaze was only on me. "You ran away so fast. I wanted to be sure you were okay."

Russian.

His accent was definitely Russian.

That was my assessment based on the acquired knowledge that came with twenty years of watching TV and movies.

"I-I'm fine."

"You're Jasmine Renner."

My frightened gaze went to Camila.

She disconnected our elbows and offered her hand. "She is, and I'm Camila Luciano. You are?"

Ignoring Camila's hand, he brought his fingers to my cheek. "More interested in talking to Jasmine."

I jumped back from his touch.

Camila moved forward. "Now isn't a good time. We really shouldn't keep our bodyguards waiting."

Releasing my cheek, the man reached for the doorjamb, blocking me with his tall, muscled body. Caged near the wall, the air around us filled with a fog of his musky, spicy cologne. He was close—too close.

His voice reverberated through me in an uneasy way. "The last time I saw you, you were kissing a man, one from a cartel, I believe."

Saw me—kissing.

He saw me kiss Rei at the Green Lady Lounge.

My mouth went dry. "I think you're mistaken."

He shook his head. "Never lie to me. I'm not mistaken. That kiss was very rememberable."

The shuffle of shoes on the hallway floor caused the man to turn. With a feigned grin, he took a step back and lifted his hands as if to surrender. Giovanni and Piero were approaching fast, their guns drawn.

"There's no need for that," the man said. He took a step back. "Once you're with me, you'll forget ever kissing anyone else."

"She's never going to kiss you," Camila said.

Piero came to my side. "We should get you back home."

The two guards holstered their guns.

The man disappeared around the corner.

I blinked as the fog of the unknown man dissipated and my bodyguard came into view. "Who was he?"

It wasn't Piero who answered. It was Giovanni.

"Zhdan Myshkin."

Camila slapped Giovanni's arm. "How did you let him get so close to Jasmine?"

"Ma'am, we didn't see him until he had taken the seat."

I reached for Camila. "Stop. It's not their fault. I think I want that second margarita."

"Jasmine," Piero said, "I think it's best if we go back to the penthouse. Contessa can make you a margarita."

"No." I swallowed and stood straighter. "Zhdan is gone. Camila and I want margaritas, don't we?"

She grinned. "More now than ever."

We walked back into the bar and retook our seats.

"*Dos más*," Camila said to the bartender.

This time, he looked past us to Giovanni. Camila turned and lifted her eyebrows at her bodyguard who then nodded to the bartender.

Giggling, I lowered my chin and reached for my mostly finished drink. When Camila swiveled toward me, I whispered, "You're my hero." I licked some of the salt from the rim before slurping the last little bit of my melted drink. "I'm glad we're getting another."

Camila lowered her voice. "Seriously, I've watched my mom and sister be the best dutiful wives and submissive women...Don't get me wrong. A little submission in the bedroom is great, especially when you love and trust the man in control. While I may be living their lives, I'm not living it the way they have. Dante appreciates my opinion. He's the one who told Giovanni to do as I say." She leaned closer. "Girl, the power is a bit intoxicating."

I chewed on my lower lip as two more margaritas arrived. "Does that mean if you say this isn't our only stop, we could go somewhere else?"

Camila scrunched her nose. "After that encounter with Zhdan, do you want to go anywhere else?"

"It's over. He's not coming back." I shrugged. "Why not?"

CHAPTER

SEVENTEEN

Reinaldo

The cartel plane touched down at the small airport east of Kansas City, the same airport where we'd landed in the past. Since the alliance was first brokered, it seemed as if this was becoming a usual stop. That said, there was nothing usual about this trip. I was here for one reason: to get Jasmine. I wasn't naïve enough to assume my goal would be reached without a fight.

Diego and Felipe, the two guards I brought with me from Sacramento flanked me, one in the front and the other in the back, as we descended the stairs, stepping into the cool late-winter air.

It was nearly one in the afternoon. Peering over the tarmac, I saw the Missouri sky was filled with shades of gray. The whole world looked monochrome, trees

145

waiting to bud and dormant grass waiting for the sun to bring it back to life. The scene was a stark contrast to Northern California. Even in the winter, our sky was blue and trees green.

The car Diego secured was waiting near the hangar. After a thorough check of the vehicle, Diego drove, and Felipe sat beside him in the front seat. I should have slept on the airplane. I didn't. Instead, I did more research into the connection between Kostya Myshkin and Leah Renner.

The capo wouldn't like my findings.

His amicability wasn't my concern. Jasmine's safety was.

The deal Dario thought he brokered with Myshkin was a sham. He needed to see that the bratva was double-crossing him before it was too late.

There was one place I knew without a doubt Jasmine would be safe—out on Bella. *Mí padre's* floating mansion was as secure as Fort Knox, if not more so.

"Straight to the penthouse," I said. "There's no use being secretive." I considered entering with guns blazing. However, I knew my lack of sleep wasn't helping my judgment.

The phone in my pocket vibrated. Jano's name was on the screen.

I answered, doubting this would be a productive conversation. "*Hola.*"

"Where the fuck have you been? I've been trying to reach you."

"I was in the plane. Had my phone off."

"Fuck, Rei. The compound in Culiacán was attacked."

His announcement rang in my ears.

The compound.

Our parent's home.

"Mama and *Padre*?" I asked.

"On Bella. *Padre está lívido.* He wants us all out on Bella immediately. He's called for a counter strike on Herrera's compound outside México City."

"Tell me about the attack."

"Gunmen took out most of the staff. There were explosions."

I shook my head. "I'm not leaving Kansas City without Jasmine."

"Fuck," Jano barked. "You're in Kansas City? I should be with you."

"I don't need a babysitter."

"Like hell you don't." His voice was raised. "Our world is exploding, and you're storming off to fucking Kansas."

"It's Missouri, asshole." I watched the growingly familiar scenes pass by the car windows. "What would you do if you had reason to believe Mia was in danger?" I didn't give him a chance to answer. "You'd burn the fucking world down—scorch it. Admit that I'm right."

"Fuck you."

"I didn't tell you I was coming here because even if you wanted to be with me to hold my hand—"

"To save you from blowing up the alliance."

"Yeah," I said. "Whatever. Even if you think you should be with me, I know you wouldn't leave Mia, and I didn't want to put you on the spot. Little Reinaldo is coming soon. You can't miss the big day."

Jano and Mia had been tight-lipped on the gender and name of their upcoming bundle of joy. No matter how many times I brought it up, my brother didn't take the bait.

"She's still a month out. I'm getting her out to Bella. If I must have a fucking obstetrician on the superyacht, I will." Jano sighed. "Listen." His tone was calmer. "I spoke to *Papá*. He's good with you marrying Jasmine with the capo's approval. He said the capo won't budge. Keeps saying she's not a Luciano."

My grip tightened on the phone. "I'm so fucking tired of hearing that. I don't give a damn about her name or her past." My thoughts went to the last time I was with her, in her bedroom. I told her she was mine. And then as time passed with no contact, I wondered if I should have said more. "Mia said you proposed."

"I did. We're married."

"You were going to marry anyway."

"I proposed." Jano chuckled. "She said no."

A scoff came from my lips, a bit of humor to take a chunk out of the palpable tension currently filling me with dread. "I want to marry her. But first, I want to be sure she's safe from Myshkin. I don't know why the capo brought Jasmine back to Kansas City with her mother there. She was safer in New York."

Out of the frying pan and into the fire.

"In New York, she had Piero," my brother said. "With the capo, she has an army."

"I don't like it." Something felt off. "There's no place safer than Bella. I filled the capo in on some things I found connecting Jasmine's mother with

Myshkin. I'm on my way to the penthouse, and I'll bring Jasmine back with me, with or without the capo's approval."

"If you deflower his princess before your wedding, that knife he threatened you with—yeah, he'll use it."

"I'd hate to make Cat a widow."

"Fuck." Jano let out a frustrated growl. "No knives. No guns."

"No weapons," I agreed. "Either she is his princess, or she isn't. He can't have it both ways."

"Call me before you leave Kansas City."

"*Sí jefe.*"

My next call was to Dante. With each ring of the unanswered call, my nerves tightened to the point of snapping. The call went to his voicemail. "Fuck."

In ten more minutes, we'd arrive at the parking garage. That was the first point of entry. I'd counted on Dante to get me into the capo's home. If Dante wasn't my answer, I had no alternative but to call the capo himself.

He answered right away. "Reinaldo, I'm sorry to hear about your father's home."

Yeah, I hadn't really processed that. "Herrera is getting too bold."

"I spoke to *el Patrón* earlier. I don't think there's anything you and I need to discuss."

My jaw clenched. "Did you review the information I sent you regarding Leah Renner and Myshkin?"

"I have."

It was like pulling fucking teeth. No, I'd done that. This was more difficult. "And your conclusion?"

"I'm speaking with Kostya this afternoon. I'll know more then."

"Where? In your office?"

"That's not information I choose to share."

"Send me a fucking passcode. I'm seven minutes from your building."

His voice slowed in a threatening manner. "You wasted a trip. Go do your job in California."

"Your alliance with Myshkin is a sham. It's fucking fragile, and you're the one getting played. If you want to keep the alliance with the Roríguez cartel, you'll let me up that fucking elevator."

"Aléjandro may have permission to speak for Jorge. That doesn't transfer to you. You're third, not second."

"I'm coming up. Either I take out a few of your guards and make my way up or we communicate like men. Send me the damn passcode." I hit the red button as my vision seeped with bright fire-engine-red rage. "Asshole."

Willing my heart not to beat out of my chest, I checked my gun and secured my knives as I waited. It took nearly five minutes, but finally the text message arrived.

I let out a long breath. "We have the passcode."

My next move was a text message to Jasmine.

"I'm on my way to the penthouse. You're leaving with me."

CHAPTER

EIGHTEEN

Reinaldo

"Weapons," the famiglia guard said, standing by the elevator in the parking garage.

Begrudgingly, I handed over my gun and two knives. I still had one blade strapped to my ankle in case of emergency. Thankfully, the guard was too busy gathering Diego's and Felipe's guns to question my honesty. It wasn't a matter of being truthful, simply deceitful through omission.

We entered the elevator, and the guard flashed his card, whisking us up into the Kansas City skyline. No one spoke as the testosterone emanated through the air, clenched jaws, balled fists, and tightened muscles abounded. If we were any less human, we'd be pissing on the walls.

The elevator doors opened.

A quick scan of the foyer filled me with disappointment. Jasmine wasn't waiting for my arrival. The tall guard at Dario's office door stood to attention as we neared. He and the elevator guard exchanged a few words, too inaudible for me to hear.

I spoke to Diego and Felipe. *"Quédate afuera."*

They both nodded, accepting my order to remain outside the capo's office. Speaking in Spanish was my way of showing the famiglia who was superior.

The tall guard opened the door, pushing it inward. With a dip of my chin, I stepped through the threshold. The capo sat behind his desk, not unlike the way I'd seen him numerous times. As the door closed, a flash to my left caught my attention. I saw the assailant out of the corner of my eye before spinning and facing him head-on.

There wasn't time to call for my guards. This was my fight.

The attacker was young and cocky.

Fuck him.

He swung his knife, swiping the air.

Grabbing his wrist, I took him down to the floor. My knee landed on his chest as I secured his knife at his neck, a trail of blood trickling from where I nicked his flesh. The entire episode took only seconds.

"Stop," the capo said. He stood from his chair. "Impressive, Reinaldo."

The knife stayed at the kid's throat. "Should I expect more of your soldiers to come from passages behind the bookcases or maybe through the door?"

Dario gestured with his chin. "Let him up."

Gritting my teeth, I did as he said. The kid gasped as I stood to my feet. "I expected more from you, capo. You want to cut me, do it yourself." I forced a grin. "Didn't I hear at one time you had the nickname *The Blade*? What's the matter, too old now?"

The capo scoffed. "If I wanted you cut, I would have done it myself." He tilted his head toward the door, wordlessly telling the kid to leave.

The kid opened his palm.

I looked at the knife in my hand and back to him. "I'll give it back when I leave."

"You'll give it back now," the capo said.

I sheathed the blade in my empty holster and took a seat across from the giant desk. Leaning back, I crossed my ankle over my knee. "Where is Jasmine?"

"She's out."

My boots slammed onto the floor as I stood. "What the fuck? You know it isn't safe for her out there."

He lifted his hand. "You wanted to talk to me man-to-man." He sat in his big leather chair. "Then talk like a man, not a hotheaded kid."

"Does she have Piero with her?"

The capo nodded. "Camila is also with her, which means Giovanni is also there."

I exhaled and sat. "My parents are out on Bella. I'm going to take Jasmine out there. She isn't safe in Kansas City, and you know it." I narrowed my eyes. "What does Myshkin have on you that you would be willing to sacrifice Jasmine?"

Dario laid his hands flat on the top of his desk. His

dark gaze burned with intensity as he stared in my direction. "I don't owe you an explanation, but I'll give you a history lesson. The war with Myshkin began between my father and Smirnov long before you were born. It's an ongoing nuisance, like a fucking splinter under your fingernail. You want to deal with bigger issues, but it's always there, irritating, annoying, distracting. In reality, we'd agreed to cohabitate in the city before the alliance with Roríguez put us in Herrera's crosshairs. Herrera offered Myshkin the famiglia's territory if he helped eliminate us. Eliminating Herrera is a better answer."

"You think that you can partner with both us and Myshkin?"

He continued to stare at me.

"You can't. No man can serve two masters. Either you will hate one and love the other, or you will be devoted to one and despise the other."

"Quoting the Bible?"

"If the verse fits."

"I'm not the servant in this scenario."

"You are," I said. "Myshkin can't eliminate Herrera. He's playing you. He wants you to get comfortable with this agreement, and when you're distracted with Herrera, he'll double-cross you. The information I sent you shows that he's been working on this plan since last October. Hell, probably before. That's where Leah Renner comes in. Why else would Myshkin give a fuck if she rots in prison? He sees a use for her."

"I've given him my word," the capo said.

"You gave *mí padre* your word."

"Jasmine isn't a—"

I was back on my feet. "Don't fucking say that again." I pointed in his direction. "Why is Piero with Jasmine?"

"To keep her safe."

"Why does he travel to New York with her?"

"Same reason."

"Why did you bring her back to Kansas City?"

He nodded. "I care about her."

"Then stop fucking disrespecting her. Either she's your princess or she's not. I don't mean by blood. I mean in your cold, dead heart."

His voice cooled to a degree above frozen. "I'm not the one who took her into public and kissed her, made a spectacle of her. That was disrespecting."

It was suddenly difficult to swallow. "I won't deny it. I kissed her. Jasmine is a beautiful and sensual woman."

"Stop."

Furrowing my brow, I narrowed my eyes. "Why is that difficult for you to face? Fuck, in the last two months, you've had three men make offers for her."

His nostrils flared. "Is that it, Reinaldo? Is this a pissing contest? Do you want Jasmine, or do you not want anyone else to have her?"

"It's not a contest. I want her, and *sí*, the thought of anyone else touching her is unfathomable." I opened my eyes wider. "Have you spoken to Zhdan Myshkin in person?"

"No, I've negotiated with Kostya."

"I'm man enough to face you in your home." I pulled the kid's knife from my holster and laid it on top of the big desk. "I surrendered my weapons. I took down your soldier. I'm the one who will walk through the gates of hell for Jasmine." When he didn't respond, I went on. "You don't want to see Myshkin's double cross, but I see it. I also know the famiglia and cartel have proven themselves to one another time after time. Fuck, Jano and Mia's baby is due in a month. Giving Jasmine to me will further cement our alliance. Don't you want to look into your wife's and daughter's eyes and know that you've done all you can for both legacies?" The capo looked as if he were about to explode. Yet I didn't stop. "Or are you willing to risk all that's been accomplished for a pipe dream of losing a fucking splinter?"

The door to the office opened and the tall guard from outside came rushing in. I stood, reaching for the knife I had just laid on the desk.

"What is it?" the capo asked.

"Mr. Luciano is on the phone." He handed Dario a cell phone.

"What?"

The capo's face went absolutely ashen. "Fuck. Is she all right?"

My pulse kicked up.

She?

She who?

He closed his eyes as his nostrils flared. "Bring her home immediately, and Dante... find out who is responsible. I want their head." He handed the phone back to the guard and focused his attention on me. "Camila and Jasmine were out to lunch." He shook his head. "All I know is they were drinking margaritas—"

"She's only twenty."

"Their lunch went well. Zhdan approached Jasmine."

"The fuck?" I was back on my feet.

"He left the restaurant. When the ladies went back to finish their meal, Jasmine became ill and disoriented. They have her in the car on the way back here."

"She was roofied?" My fingers balled into fists. "I'll kill him."

Dario exhaled. "If I asked you to leave—"

"I'd tell you to go fuck yourself."

Slowly, the capo stood. "You may stay as long as you agree to my rules."

My lips formed a straight line. I would listen.

"You will respect me as capo dei capi and as Jasmine's guardian. That means you'll clean up the way you talk to me."

If that meant I could stay here, I could agree. "Is there more?"

"I need to find out what's happening with Myshkin. In the meantime, the only way I'll allow you to take Jasmine to the safety of your father's yacht is if she's married. It's bad enough that you've kissed."

"You'll agree to allow us to marry?"

"Your theory has merit. I won't use Jasmine. You obviously care for her."

My shoulders relaxed for the first time since I boarded the plane. "I do, sir."

CHAPTER

NINETEEN

Jasmine

A wave of nausea ripped me from my sleep. I sat up, dazed as I looked around my bedroom. My mind whirled with questions as I threw back the covers and hurried toward the bathroom. Falling to my knees, I retched as the contents of my stomach came back up my throat.

"You're going to be okay," the female voice said softly while gentle hands gathered my hair.

My entire body trembled as I peered over my shoulder to see Catalina. Before I could speak, another wave of nausea hit me like a punch to the stomach. The vomit reeked, splattering into the water and leaving my mouth tasting horrible. Shaking, I flushed the toilet and laid my forehead on the edge of the toilet seat as I tried to remember coming home.

"What happened?" I finally asked.

"Someone roofied you," she said, kneeling at my side. "Do you remember anything from lunch?"

I pushed myself to stand, using the walls for support and moved slowly toward the vanity. Pain radiated from my stomach, making it feel as if someone were wringing it out—twisting it. Through bloodshot eyes, I stared in the mirror. My reflection was as pitiful as I felt. Red hair messed, and my complexion pale. Reaching for the cup, I filled it with water, rinsed, and spat. As I was pasting my toothbrush, I remembered Catalina's question and shook my head.

"I remember eating Mexican with Camila." I spun toward Catalina. "Oh God, is Camila all right?"

"She's fine. She's worried about you, but apparently, her drink wasn't spiked."

My temples throbbed as I brushed away the horrendous taste. When I finished, I realized I was suddenly parched, drinking two glasses of water. Looking down at my clothes, I saw my jeans were gone, leaving me in panties, a bra, and the blouse I wore to lunch. I scrunched my nose at the material peppered with vomit. "I should shower."

"Can you? Do you need help?" She feigned a smile. "I can get Contessa if you'd rather have her."

Shaking my head caused my temples to revolt. I shut my eyes, inhaled, and opened them. "I think I'm okay." I lifted a few strands of my hair. "This is gross." I looked at Catalina. "Who did this to me?"

"Dario and Dante are on it. They'll find out."

I pulled my shirt over my head. After turning on the

shower, I met Catalina's gaze. "Will you stay here? I'm kind of shaky."

"Of course."

Removing the rest of my clothes, I stepped into the shower and lifted my face to the spray. "I don't remember anything," I said, speaking louder, "after we went back to the bar." My hand went to the shower wall for support. "I remember something from before that."

"What?" Catalina asked.

"Zhdan Myshkin was there. He sat next to me at the bar. He tried to talk to me." The memories came rushing back. "He touched me, cornered me as I was leaving the bathroom." My cheeks rose if only for a second. "Camila told him I'd never kiss him and then Piero and Giovanni —they had guns."

"Did they shoot?"

"No, Zhdan left." I poured a dollop of shampoo into my palm and worked the lather through my hair. The sweet scent of jasmine and honeysuckle was a welcome change. After conditioning my hair, I sat on the seat and rested as the warm spray continued to rain down.

"Are you going to be able to finish?"

"Yes. I just need a second."

As I again lifted my face to the spray, tears prickled the back of my eyes. "Dario must be furious."

"He's worried. I just sent him a text message telling him you're awake and showering."

After rinsing the bodywash from my flesh and conditioner from my hair, I turned off the water. As Catalina handed me a plush towel, I asked, "Were you afraid of marrying Dario?"

Her eyes opened wide.

"You didn't know him at all," I prompted.

Catalina nodded. "I was terrified."

"And still, you did it. You married him. Why?"

Her smile grew. "I was wrong to be terrified. Dario is a good man and a good husband."

"Zhdan scares me."

She inhaled. "This is probably the time to tell you that you have a visitor downstairs."

Stepping out of the shower, I wrapped myself in the towel and looked at myself in the mirror. A visitor. Zhdan had said something about me kissing him.

Is he here?

"I'm obviously not up for visitors." I looked around, noticing the window for the first time. The sun had set, leaving the sky dark. "What time is it?"

Catalina glanced at her watch. "It's nearly nine."

"I've been passed out since what…?"

"They brought you home after two."

"Piero saved me again."

"We're very grateful you didn't try to ditch him. His and Giovanni's quick thinking got you out of the restaurant."

"Did they carry me?"

"You walked."

Catalina and I both turned toward the bathroom door, to see Camila.

"You walked," she repeated, "but you were talking oddly. You were laughing and then crying."

I exhaled. "I'm so sorry."

Camila came into the bathroom and hugged me.

"Jasmine, I'm sorry. It was my idea to go out and to have margaritas."

"If someone wanted to roofie Jasmine," Catalina said, "they could have put it in her water. Although, neither of you are old enough to drink alcohol."

Camila pressed her lips together and smiled.

"That bartender," I said, "he did this to me?"

"Dante is getting video footage of the restaurant. The bartender has denied any involvement."

After running a comb through my wet hair, I turned to Camila. "Who is my visitor?"

"She doesn't know?" Camila asked. "I figured that's why you showered."

"I showered because I stank." I scrunched my nose. "Did I vomit earlier?"

Camila nodded. "In the car."

My shoulders drooped. "Oh, I need to tell Giovanni I'm sorry."

"He said it was good that you were getting the drugs out of your system." She waved her hand in front of her nose. "I don't think I'll be craving Mexican food for a while."

"This is embarrassing."

"No," Catalina said, "you didn't roofie yourself. You have no reason to be embarrassed. Now, I suggest getting dressed before going downstairs."

My hands still trembled. "Can my visitor come up here?"

"Definitely not," Catalina said. "Besides Contessa is champing at the bit to feed you."

"Food?"

"Something bland," Camila said. "It'll make you feel better, or at least that's what Dante said. I'm not a real expert on these things."

Catalina went toward the door. "I'll go let Contessa and Dario know you're on your way down."

After I slipped on panties, leggings, my bra, and a long sweater, I went back to the bathroom. While I was securing my wet hair into a low ponytail, Camila leaned against the doorjamb.

"I really am sorry."

I shrugged. "I don't remember acting like a fool."

"You weren't a fool. You were talking about Rei. In the car you were asking Piero and Giovanni if they'd help you escape to California."

I lifted my hands to my face. "Oh, I'm embarrassed."

"Dante said that the drug lowers inhibitions, kind of like a truth serum."

"Does that mean I wanted to escape Dario and go to California? Or was I just terrified of Zhdan?"

"I guess we'll find out," she said, "when we go downstairs."

"Why?"

"Rei is your visitor."

My eyes opened wide. "Oh shit. I can't go downstairs like this."

"He was waiting in the garage for you when you arrived covered in vomit. If that didn't scare him away, the clean version won't."

I leaned against the vanity and sighed. "Rei saw me like that."

She nodded. "He also heard when you told him you

wanted him and to do whatever..." She furrowed her brow. "Let me remember. You wanted him to do whatever was in his text messages you never received."

Wrapping my arms around my midsection, I winced. "I think I might be sick again." My fingers felt cooler than a moment ago. "I can't remember any of that. The last thing I remember Zhdan left, and you and I went back to our seats."

"It wasn't long after that when you started slurring your words. At first, I thought it was a second margarita."

"Who else heard me in the garage?"

"Giovanni, Piero, me, oh...and Dario."

My knees gave out as I slid to the floor. "I can't leave this bedroom, ever."

"You can. I don't know what Rei said or did, but Dante said Dario is giving him another chance."

"Really?" My eyes opened wide. "And he wants it after seeing me so...awful?"

"Let's go downstairs and find out."

CHAPTER

TWENTY

Reinaldo

’d spent the last seven hours worried sick about Jasmine. The things she’d said when she saw me in the garage were completely out of character and at the same time, sexy as hell. I knew enough about La Rocha, or Rohypnol, to know its effects. By the time they got Jasmine to the apartment, she was coming down from the initial high. Some people purposely took the drug for that high. When it was mixed with alcohol, it exacerbated the alcohol’s intoxication.

As Piero helped her from the car, I didn’t see the mess she’d made by getting sick. It was her fucking blue eyes. They spun, unable to truly focus until they landed on me.

“Rei.” She wobbled as she called out to me.

Despite the capo standing at my side, I hurried to help her.

She let go of Piero and fell into me. "Are you really here?" Her words were slurred. She slapped my chest with her hand. "I feel you." She turned to Camila. "I have a great imagination."

I wrapped my arm around her waist to keep her from falling. She stumbled with her steps. "I want to know what you said in your text messages." Her lips curled in an exaggerated smile. "What are you going to do to me? I've wondered ever since you told me."

Fuck.

The capo was listening to every word.

Jasmine pointed her finger at him. "He doesn't want me to marry you. He wants me to marry Zsa-dan, Zsa-Zen." She shook her head. "Zhdan Myshkin." She shook her head. "He scares me."

Throughout the ride, I kept her upright.

She laid her head against my shoulder. Her voice was softer. "I think I could love you." Her crystal-blue stare looked up at me. "Do you think you could love me?"

I brought my lips to her forehead. "I know I could."

Jasmine exhaled. "I'm a stray."

My forehead furrowed. "What?"

"A stray...you know...stray...unwanted."

The capo growled, but my attention was on Jasmine. "You need to rest."

Again, she tipped her chin up to me. "You said you wanted me."

"I do."

Sighing, she laid her head back on my shoulder. As the elevator doors opened, I scooped her into my arms. Her head lay back and her eyes were closed.

"Give her to me," Dario said. "I'll take her upstairs."

I hugged her against me. "I'll take her upstairs. You can come with us." I looked down at my shirt speckled with vomit. "No sense dirtying your suit."

She didn't stir as Cat pulled back the blankets and I laid her on her bed. Looking around, I saw her bedroom as I hadn't the night I'd snuck in. It was filled with bright colors, perfectly representing Jasmine's energy.

Since that time, Jasmine was checked over by the outfit's doctor. He confirmed that vomiting was her best treatment. The amount of drug she ingested would determine the length of time she was unconscious. Her vitals were good. Each time I was allowed to see her, I tried to convince myself she was merely sleeping.

Showered and dressed in Dante's clothes—Catalina took mine to wash or burn. I wasn't quite sure which— Dante, Dario, and I worked side by side to learn what we could about what exactly happened at the restaurant. When Dante gained access to the security footage we had our answer.

Before the altercation near the bathroom that Camila described, Zhdan sat at the bar in a stool at Jasmine's side. Before she noticed his presence, he pulled a capsule from his breast pocket and quickly sprinkled powder into her nearly-finished drink.

"That's why he followed her to the bathroom," Dante said. "He thought she'd consumed the roofied drink already."

"But she hadn't," I observed. "If Camila and then Giovanni and Piero hadn't followed..."

The capo shook his head.

Following the bathroom exchange, Zhdan went back to the bar. He didn't approach his seat, only gesturing to the man with him to leave.

As we rewatched the video together, at the sight of Zhdan sprinkling the drug in her drink, my blood boiled. "He's a dead man. Where can I find him?" I asked. Turning to Dario, I added, "He doesn't deserve Jasmine."

Dario nodded. "He doesn't. Do you still want her?"

I couldn't believe he would ask the question. "I wouldn't be here if I didn't." When he didn't speak, I added, "Yes. I want her. I've told her that and I meant it."

The capo defeatedly looked at Dante. "This will fuck up things with Myshkin."

"Things are fucked with him as it is."

"When she wakes," the capo said, speaking to me, "I want to talk to her. If this is what you both want, it will happen. There won't be a big wedding—not because Jasmine doesn't deserve one. A celebration would be a way to flaunt your marriage, to Myshkin. We can get a priest here tonight, and you two will be legally wed before you take her to California."

"*Mí padre* and *madre*."

The capo shook his head. "Jorge won't travel to Missouri with what happened in Culiacán. It wouldn't be safe. I won't allow you to take Jasmine unless you're married."

I stood taller. "Then we'll marry."

The next few hours were spent texting Jano, nursing a glass of bourbon, and pacing between the capo's living room and office. The man with Zhdan was identified as

Dmitri Makarova. Dario would get his head. I'd fucking deliver it on a silver platter.

Every now and then, I'd receive an update from upstairs. It was either Cat or the housekeeper. Once Camila arrived, she also kept me updated.

I turned as Cat came down the stairs. "Jasmine will be down in a minute."

My pulse jumped. "How is she?"

"She's weak and tired, but she'll be all right."

Setting my drink on a nearby table, I made my way to the bottom of the staircase. It took all my restraint not to run up the stairs and help her come down. My focus was entirely on the second level, to the point where I didn't know or care who else was waiting for her descent.

My heart hammered behind my breastbone when she came into view. She and Camila were talking but stopped when her beautiful blue stare met mine. By the time she reached the bottom of the staircase, her cheeks and neck were filled with a crimson hue.

"Rei."

I offered her my hand. Hesitantly, she took it.

"I'm sorry if I said...I don't remember—"

When her sock-covered feet landed on the main-level marble, I fell to one knee. "Jasmine, I've never lied to you. I want you as my wife. I'm not a good man. I am an honest man. I want you beside me. I want to make you happy and keep you safe. However..." —I took a breath— "I need to know that it's what you want. Will you marry me?"

Tears streamed down her cheeks as she looked around.

It was the first time I thought about having an audience.

"Is this real?" she asked, looking at someone behind me. Her attention went to me. "Yes, Rei. I want to marry you. You and only you."

I stood, still holding her hand. "I don't have a ring, but we'll get one, the biggest diamond you've ever seen."

She shook her head. "I don't need a big diamond. I just want you." She pushed up on her tiptoes, but before her lips met mine, the capo cleared his throat. We both turned to him.

"Jasmine, we have some miscommunication to discuss."

Shyly smiling, she took a step back. "When? When will we marry?"

"Tonight, *preciosa*."

"Tonight?"

"I guess it depends on what happens during your discussion with the capo."

Biting her lip, she nodded and hurried toward Dario's office.

Dante came forward and patted my shoulder. "Huge cajones. Enormous."

"Didn't realize there was an audience."

He retrieved my unfinished glass of bourbon and brought it to me. "Giant."

CHAPTER

TWENTY-ONE

Jasmine

Dario waited by the door. As soon as I entered, he closed it. Instead of sitting behind his desk, he took the chair to my side as I sat in the same place where only a day ago, I'd learned my fate with Zhdan. This felt different. For what seemed like an eternity, silence reigned. It wasn't uncomfortable, more like a warm blanket on a cool night.

"I owe you an apology," he said.

"Why?"

"The things you were saying earlier—"

I covered my face with my hands. "Oh, I'm so embarrassed." Peeking over the tips of my fingers, I met his gaze. "I don't remember any of it."

Dario inhaled. "I remember and I'm sorry I made you feel the way I did. It wasn't my intention." He reached

173

out, laying his hand on my knee. "You should never consider yourself a stray."

Sitting taller, I gasped. "Dario, I wouldn't use that word. I know how upset it made you and Josie."

He took his hand away. "You did. In the elevator talking to Reinaldo, you used the word stray and..." He exhaled. "I was wrong to deny your marriage to Reinaldo. He obviously cares for you, and you are a worthy offering. He's also right that you'll be safe with his parents."

My eyes opened wide. "With his parents? In Mexico?"

The side of his lips quirked. "Sort of. I'm sure he'll explain it." His dark eyes filled with concern. "Is this what you want?"

"What I want?" I nodded. "When I'm with Rei, I feel special. He's possessive and intense and instead of those qualities scaring me, I like them."

Dario nodded. "I'm sorry to make you feel like you're unworthy, Jasmine. You deserve to be happy and loved. It's all Josie ever wanted for you. I should have adopted you instead of asking for guardianship."

It was my turn to reach out. I laid my hand on his knee. "I don't care what my last name has been. It's going to change" —I lifted my eyebrows in question— "tonight?"

"Yes. What about classes?"

"There's a good chance my professors will allow me to finish the semester online. After that, I can enroll in California."

Dario covered my hand with his. "I'm proud of you, Jasmine. I always have been. If you'll allow me, I'd like to walk you to Reinaldo—give you away." He forced a smile. "But not really. It's a tradition. Just know that no matter what the circumstances or situation, you have a home here in Kansas City with Catalina and me." He squeezed my hand. "By definition, a stray is homeless, wandering from place to place."

Fighting back the tears, I nodded. "I'm not a stray."

Dario began to stand.

"What will happen with Myshkin? Will this cause problems?"

"Not your concern."

"My mother?" I asked.

"Go with Reinaldo and be safe. If she's genuine in her desire to see you, then you can decide when that happens. If she isn't, then go on with your life. Josie was more of a mother than Leah will ever be. Remember what Josie wanted for you."

I nodded. "To be happy and loved."

He walked around to the other side of his desk. "I'm going to tell you something that may or may not be useful in your marriage."

Sitting taller on the edge of the chair, I waited.

"Men like me, and perhaps Reinaldo, can be both fearless and terrified."

My eyebrows knitted together. "I don't understand."

"You're not supposed to. From a young age I was expected to exude confidence and face down any enemy. I was taught to never trust and always be suspicious. There was no opponent I couldn't conquer. And at the same time, I failed miserably when it came to my personal life." Dario opened a side drawer on his desk and brought out a small box. "Not too long after you and Josie came to live with me, I bought this." He pushed the box toward me. "I always planned that one day…" He inhaled deeply. "You see, as confident as I was, I couldn't face down the one man who never wanted happiness for me." He jutted his chin. "Open it."

He was talking about his father.

Slowly, I reached for the box, unsure of what I'd find. Lifting the lid, I found a velvet-covered jewelry box. My stomach twisted as I opened the hinged top. "Oh, Dario." The ring inside was stunning and simple. A gold band with a round diamond. I wasn't a judge of precious stones, but I would guess two or three carats. My gaze met his as tears prickled the back of my eyes. "You bought this for Josie?"

He nodded. "One day never came."

"Catalina? She should have it."

Dario shook his head. "Catalina's ring is a family heirloom. I told her today about the ring and my idea for you to have it. She agreed without hesitation."

"What? You want me to have it?"

"Even though I was never brave enough to give it to her, it's a part of your sister. If you don't want it…"

I hugged the box to my chest. "I do."

"You should have a ring when you're married." He reached forward. "I'll give it to Reinaldo." A smile cracked his veneer. "You deserve a big wedding."

Closing the lid, I handed the box back to Dario. "I don't care about the wedding. I care about who I'm marrying." My stomach growled and I quickly laid my hand over it.

"Contessa has food for you in the kitchen. You should eat and then...your wedding."

I looked down at my leggings and sweater. "I need to change."

"That's up to you. Dante is in charge of getting the priest here tonight."

My eyes opened wide. "Oh my God. I'm really getting married."

His cheeks rose in an unusually pronounced grin. "You are."

The next hour flew by. Contessa had a variety of options for me when it came to food. I settled on scrambled eggs, toast, and fruit. I'd been asleep long enough to feel like it was morning instead of nearing midnight.

Catalina, Contessa, and Camila gathered with me in my bedroom to help me prepare. A thorough inspection of the dresses hanging in my closet sent both Catalina and Camila to their own closets for options.

"I doubt I'll fit in any of Camila's clothes," I said to Contessa when we were alone. Peering down, I smiled. "I'm more endowed than she is."

Contessa reached for my hand. "I'm sorry."

Tonight must be the night for apologies.

"Why?"

"The things I said about Mr. Roríguez and Mr. Ruiz on Christmas Eve. I was wrong to judge them. Today, I've watched him. He's a strong man and still he was racked with worry about you." She nodded. "He cares for you."

"I care for him, too."

"Will you forgive me?"

I wrapped my arms around her shoulders. "I did a long time ago."

Contessa wiped away a tear from her cheek. "I'm going to put together a wedding reception. If only you would have given me more time."

"We don't need a reception."

She waved me off, nearly colliding with Catalina in the doorway.

"I found these," Catalina said, carrying an armload of white dresses. "If you'd like" —she dropped the others on my bed and pulled out her wedding dress— "you could wear this."

I gasped, remembering how beautiful she looked during their wedding. Running my fingers over the white material, I assessed the flowing skirt, chapel-length train, a sweetheart neckline, a shape-forming bodice, and a long line of pearl buttons down the back.

Camila appeared in the doorway with her own load of dresses in all colors. "You had it repaired," she said to Catalina.

Catalina rolled her eyes. "Arianna had it repaired." She held up the bodice. "You can't tell it was ripped."

"Dario ripped it?" I asked.

"No. Arianna and Francesca did." She stood straighter. "It's a long story. What's important is that it is repaired and well, I won't be wearing it again."

"What about Ariadna Gia?"

"Rei won't cut it off of you," Catalina said. "If she's interested in forty years when her father allows her to marry, we can worry about it then."

Forty years.

That may be wishful thinking.

I took the dress from Catalina and stood before the full-length mirror. Holding the beautiful dress up to myself, I asked, "Do you think it will fit?"

Camila dropped her dresses on my bed. "Probably better than any of mine. You have boobs."

The room filled with laughter.

It was hard to believe that hours ago I'd been roofied and now...I sighed. "I'd like to try it on."

"May I help with your hair?" Camila asked. "I love the color and curls."

Swallowing, I tilted my head. "I know it may be weird, since you two were supposed to wed, but would you stand up with me, be my matron of honor?"

A giant smile came to her lips. "Yes, and I'll wear one of the dresses I brought. What color should I wear?"

Closer to midnight, Dario knocked on the door. I turned, wearing Catalina's dress, my hair pulled up with pearl combs, and my makeup hiding the earlier paleness. My gaze met his. His eyes shone as he scanned me up and down. "You're beautiful, Jasmine."

I noticed he'd changed into a fresh suit, and his face was freshly shaved. "Thank you."

"Is the priest here?" Catalina asked. Sometime while I was getting my makeup done, she'd slipped out, only to return in a cocktail dress.

"Waiting downstairs. I pulled a few strings. The license arrived via courier a few minutes ago. The only thing missing from this wedding is the bride." Dario offered me his arm.

"Oh, let us go down ahead," Catalina said, tugging Camila's hand.

Dario covered my hand resting on his arm. "If I could do it over, I'd do so many things differently with you."

I shook my head. "You gave me a life I never would have had."

"I gave more than that. I was just never brave enough to say it." Moving his arm, he wrapped my shoulders in an embrace. "You have my love."

Sniffling, I looked up at him. "Don't make me ruin this makeup."

With his lips pressed together, he nodded. "It has taken Catalina to make me understand, but Jasmine, you've had my love since the afternoon we met."

"You've had mine too."

He kissed my cheek. "Your groom is waiting."

TWENTY-TWO

Reinaldo

I stood between the priest and Dante near the floor-to-ceiling windows. Missouri's dark sky caused the panes to reflect like giant mirrors. Contessa had rearranged some of the furniture, creating a mini aisle, with two chairs on each side. Catalina sat on one side. The groom's side was empty.

My heart ached for my mother. She was sentimental about things like weddings. *Mí padre* was too busy to care. I'd talked to him after receiving the capo's blessing, and he told me to get my new bride to Bella.

Transfixed, I couldn't look away. Once again, my eyes were glued to the staircase.

After music began, Camila was the first to descend. She looked pretty in a long golden dress. For a split second, I thought how strange it was for her to be here—

a part of my wedding—considering our past. As she approached, her green eyes twinkled as they settled on the man to my side.

Jano asked me once how I felt about Camila since she and Dante married. My answer was that we were as we'd been for most of our lives. We were friends. The uncomfortable thoughts disappeared with the contentment that despite the absence of my family, Jasmine and I would wed surrounded by friends.

The music changed and Catalina stood.

My pulse raced as I looked toward the staircase.

Jasmine was an absolute vision. She was wearing a wedding dress. I wanted to ask how that was possible. Did the capo have one of those sitting around like the diamond ring Dante was now holding? But words couldn't form. I was too busy watching my bride come closer with her hand on the arm of the man she admired. Her gorgeous blue eyes stayed focused on me as if she could see the man I was and was willing to learn the husband I could be. Having her trust was as important as having her hand.

We'd taken a bumpy road to get to this point. I'd do it all over again to have Jasmine at my side.

The dress fit her curves, the bodice pushing her breasts up in a sexy yet demure way. Her fiery red hair was pulled up, revealing her slender neck and collarbones. My fingers itched to reach out, as I had the first night here in this penthouse. To touch her soft skin. Once we were safely on Bella, I would explore every valley and dip of the sensual curves currently hidden beneath the long white dress.

Their Italian tradition of cutting the wedding dress sounded better than it ever had before. I intended to expose and explore every inch of Jasmine's body to discover what brought her pleasure. And then I'd spend the rest of our lives making her scream my name in ecstasy.

When the priest asked who gave the bride, my breath caught as the capo replied, "It is with great honor that I do." Lifting her hand from his arm, he placed it in my open palm. "Take care of her."

"With my life."

Jasmine's cheeks rose as we held hands.

I supposed I should recall every word the priest said, but I didn't. It wasn't that I wasn't listening; it was more that I was in awe of where this day had landed. We both replied appropriately when asked questions. "I do. I will."

The band and diamond slipped perfectly over her finger, its significance more than any ring set we could have purchased. I offered to pay the capo and not surprisingly, he refused. I'd never have the pleasure of meeting Jasmine's sister, but the ring made it feel as if she were here.

It was when the priest said that I may kiss my bride that my tired body roared to life.

We turned to one another. Cupping her cheek, I stroked her porcelain complexion before leaning forward until our lips met. In front of God and even more importantly, in front of the capo dei capi, I staked my claim. This was our third kiss and the longer it lasted, the more I wanted. A moan escaped from her lips, reminding me that once again we had an audience.

I pulled away with a grin.

"It is my pleasure," the priest said, "in front of God and our small gathering to introduce for the first time, Mr. and Mrs. Reinaldo Roríguez."

Camila clapped.

Standing back farther in the living room, I saw Contessa wipe away a tear.

"*Señora* Roríguez," I repeated.

Jasmine held tight to my hand. "I like the way that sounds."

"Me too."

Before we could say more to one another, our gathering came to us. Camila and Catalina hugged Jasmine while Dante and Dario shook my hand.

After champagne and cake, Jasmine went upstairs to gather some of her things. Dario agreed to have the rest shipped to Sacramento.

Camila tapped me on the shoulder.

"*Sí?*"

"Your bride is upstairs, and she could use a little help getting out of that dress."

I hadn't considered her changing. "Me?" I pointed to myself and looked around for the capo.

"You're her husband," she said with a grin. "I mean, if you don't want to, I can—"

I quickly handed Camila my champagne glass and made my way up the stairs. Approaching the door, I remembered the first time I was in this bedroom with the threat of death hanging over my head. Instead of knocking, I turned the knob and pushed the door inward. Jasmine was standing in front of the full-length mirror.

She didn't know I was here. There was power in watching someone, learning their habits and their tells. I wondered what Jasmine was thinking. Did she know how she affected me? Ever since our encounter on Christmas Eve, she'd been an ongoing presence in my mind, a burning ember waiting to combust.

"Oh," she startled, spinning toward me. "I didn't hear you come in."

"I'm your husband."

Jasmine nodded, looked down at the wedding rings and back up. "It all happened so fast."

"No, *preciosa*, not fast. I've wanted you for a long time. I should have made my intentions clear long before Christmas Eve."

She tilted her head. "Before that night in the living room?"

"*Sí.*" I took a step closer. "*Mí papá* showed me a picture of you." I stepped closer, reaching for the combs holding up her hair and tugged one out. Tendrils of fiery red curls cascaded over her shoulder. "The picture did not do you justice." I reached for another comb, releasing more of her flowing mane. "That night...downstairs..." Her cobalt-blue stare was glued to me. "I knew you would be mine."

"That night you..." She inhaled. "You made me feel things I'd never felt."

Slowly walking around her, I removed the last comb, freeing the last of her luscious long hair. I stopped mere inches in front of her. "Things?"

Her pink tongue darted to her lips. "You looked at me like no one had ever looked at me."

"Am I looking at you the same way now?"

Jasmine nodded. "It's scary and at the same time exciting." She took a step back.

From my angle, I could see the long row of buttons, her flowing hair in the mirror, and her flushed, beautiful face at the same time. "I'm looking at you and thinking about all the things I want now that you're mine."

"Rei..."

Her breathing had grown shallower and the vein in her neck thumped in double time.

"I want to rip that dress off you and unwrap the greatest present I've ever received."

"The dress is Catalina's...you can't..."

Bending at the waist, I unsheathed the knife from my ankle holster.

Jasmine gasped and her eyes grew as wide as saucers.

"I want to see you as no man has seen you, Jasmine. I want to touch you where you've never been touched by anyone. The thoughts of things I want to do to you have me painfully hard."

She swallowed and closed her eyes as I brought the tip of my knife to the neckline of the dress. Dropping the blade to the floor, I wrapped her in my arms and began my assault of her slender neck. Kisses, nips, and licks, my facial hair left a reddened trail on her sensitive skin.

"Oh, Rei," she panted, reaching out to me and holding my shoulders.

"I want to taste every millimeter of you, inside and out."

Letting go of my shoulders, she stepped back, colliding with the mirror. "Rei, stop."

There was a fine line between scared and excited, a tightrope to walk. I took a step back, giving her space and lightened my tone. "Do you remember what I said to you in this bedroom before I was banished to California?"

She nodded. "You said the next time we saw one another would be our wedding."

I slapped a fist against my chest. "Señora Roríguez, I am a man of my word." I grinned. "I also said something else."

Pink filled Jasmine's cheeks. "I remember. I've relived that conversation in my mind many times."

"Say it, what I said."

She blinked before lifting her hands to my shoulders. "You said you wanted to fuck me."

"That hasn't changed, but an important fact has—you're now my wife."

"I am. I'm a little scared."

"And also excited?"

She nodded.

With my finger, I forged a trail from behind her ear to her neck, to her collarbone, and down to the apex of the neckline. "Tell me," I said, my words breathy on her sensitive skin, "have you ever relived that conversation while touching yourself?"

When I pulled away to see her face, her eyes were closed, and her lower lip was secured between her white teeth.

"*Preciosa,* you can tell me. The idea is making me hard this second."

"I have."

"Did you come?" As she tilted her chin lower, I lifted it. "Don't try to hide from me. I want to see your pleasure."

"I don't know if I have or not. It felt good, but not like they describe in books."

"When I touch you, you will know. From your head to your toes, you will know."

Fuck, the idea of her coming with thoughts of me was making me painfully hard. Cupping the back of her neck, I crashed my mouth over hers, the way I wanted to kiss her downstairs. Jasmine didn't shy away, pressing her body against mine and moaning as my tongue teased the slit of her lips. Without hesitation, she opened, allowing me entrance into her warm haven. She tasted so fucking good, like sunshine to a frozen tundra or water to a sunbaked desert. My hands roamed over her arms and down to her waist.

"I'm supposed to be helping you out of that dress." I spun her around, eyeing the long line of buttons. "Fuck, tell me there's a zipper under there."

As I bent to pick up the knife, she shook her head. "Not an option. If you don't want to help, I'll call for Camila."

"Oh, fuck that."

I moved behind her gently so as to not rip the dress and began at the top button. Releasing one after another, each one revealed more and more of her skin. Curses in Spanish and praises in English spilled from my lips as the back of the dress unfolded, exposing her spine. Finally, the dress pooled around her high-heeled shoes.

"Fuck," I murmured, as my wife stood before me in a corset, lace panties, and high heels. "You're fucking amazing."

Through the lace I saw a small patch of red hair at the apex of her legs.

"Who has seen what I'm seeing?"

"No one—no man."

"I want to fuck you, Jasmine. I'm not going to do it in your childhood bedroom with your family downstairs."

She let out a breath.

"When we're on Bella, I will make you completely mine."

"I'm yours, Rei." Her eyes widened. "We don't have to rush. We have forever."

What did she say?

"Fucking my wife after our wedding isn't rushing."

"What is Bella?"

CHAPTER
TWENTY-THREE

Jasmine

I woke, momentarily unsure of my surroundings. Even before opening my eyes, Rei's sandalwood-and-leather scent permeated my senses. Blinking, I found I'd fallen asleep with my head on his hard shoulder. A quick glance at my watch told me we were approximately three hours into our three-and-a-half-hour flight.

With the time change, it would only be two thirty in the morning when we landed. As I lifted my head, Rei stirred. He must have fallen asleep with his arm protectively around me. Bravely, I brought my finger to his handsome face and ran it over his cheekbones. He was my husband. In near slumber, he wasn't as intense.

Rei blinked.

"You're real." I lifted my hand with the wedding rings

and splayed my fingers. "When I first woke, I was afraid yesterday was a dream, and maybe I'd be back in my bedroom alone."

His voice rumbled with sleepiness. "No, *preciosa*. Your nights of sleeping alone are over."

Sleeping was acceptable. It was what came before it that had me worried.

The arm that had been around me pulled me closer, flattening my breasts against his muscular chest. "Mine," he growled seconds before his lips came to mine.

A bolt of electricity sizzled through my nervous system, synapse after synapse sparking to life. I wasn't sure how he could do it, but with simply a kiss and being pressed against his hardness, untouched parts of my body began to warm and tingle. Unapologetically, his tongue sought entrance, dancing and tangoing with mine. When I pulled back, my lips felt bruised and swollen in the best of ways. My tongue darted out to ease the tenderness.

Rei's eyes hooded as he cupped my chin and ran his thumb over my lips. "I need to be easier on you. Your lips aren't used to being kissed."

"I'm not breakable. And I like the way you kiss me."

"Good, because I plan to do a lot more of it."

As I attempted to push away and stand, Rei reached for my hand. "Are you trying to leave me already? You might want to wait until we land."

I shook my head. "I don't want to leave you. I need to use the bathroom."

His lips twitched. "We could become members of the mile-high club. I could bend you over the sink and—"

The sound of throat clearing stopped his sentence.

One of the women who greeted us earlier entered the cabin. "Señor and Señora Roríguez, please secure your seat belts, we're preparing to land."

I almost giggled at Rei's exaggerated expression of disappointment. "Do I have time...?" I gestured toward the bathroom.

"Yes, ma'am. Please hurry."

As I turned, I saw Diego and Felipe, Rei's soldiers he'd brought to Kansas City, sitting near the front of the plane, separated from us by a curtain. Warmth filled my cheeks, wondering what they heard.

I quickly did my business and returned to the cabin. The seat beside my husband's was where I belonged. After I secured my seat belt, Rei again reached for my hand. "I can't wait for you to meet *mí madre*." He sounded the happiest I'd heard him. "She will love you from the moment she sees you."

"We met briefly at Christmas."

"*Sí*, but then you were not my wife."

"You haven't told me about Bella." There were so many things we didn't know about one another. "What and where is it?"

"She's right now off the coast of California near San Diego. Mama wants to be near when Jano's baby is born."

"So, Bella is a boat?"

Rei grinned. "*Sí*, a big boat. I told you to bring a bathing suit." His smile faded as he leaned his head back on the leather seat. "I'd not thought about it until now, but it seems that Bella is now my parents' home."

"I thought they lived in Mexico."

His jaw clenched, the muscles in his cheeks pulling tight. "A few days ago, their home, where Jano and I were raised, was attacked. Many of the house staff were killed. I don't know how much damage was done to the structure. Jano said there were explosions."

This was real life—now mine.

No wonder Rei was so intense.

With each word, my eyes grew bigger, and my lips opened. "Who would do that?"

"Elizondro Herrera. He wants to take over the Roríguez cartel. Hasn't the capo told you anything about the war?"

I shook my head. "He's used the word *war*, but I thought it was all about the bratva in Kansas City." The name tasted sour on my lips. "Myshkin. But your parents, thankfully, weren't hurt."

"I guess we could say that Jano's baby saved them."

"You keep saying that. I think Mia has had something to do with the baby too."

His smile returned. "You're right."

The hum of landing gear lowering filled the plane. I gripped the arms of the chair, my knuckles blanching.

Rei prized my fingers away from the seat and held my hand. "We're safe."

I nodded. "It's the takeoffs and landings that I don't like."

"How do you feel about helicopters?"

My eyes nearly bugged out. "Why?"

"Because we'll be flying in a helicopter to Bella. It's better than a boat at night."

I leaned back against the seat, contemplating the abrupt change of course my life had taken. Less than twenty-four hours ago, I was having lunch with Camila. Since that time, I was roofied, proposed to, married—to a man I hardly knew—flown to California, and was about to take a helicopter into the Pacific Ocean to stay on a drug lord's boat.

"*Preciosa*, are you okay?"

"It's been a lot for one day." I met his gaze. "I've never been on a helicopter."

"I predict you will have many firsts."

My core twisted as my nerves prickled. It wasn't like I wasn't expecting sex. Rei told me he wanted me that way the night he was in my bedroom. That didn't mean I wasn't both nervous and excited. Camila made it sound like sex was the greatest thing in the world. There was no doubt my body responded to Rei. It had since that unexpected meeting in Dario's living room.

That subject was put on hold as Diego drove us to a large mansion. "Whose house is this?" I asked, entering their gates around three in the morning.

"Nicolas Ruiz. We won't bother them. They have a helipad, and this is where we'll be picked up."

Helipad.

"You were serious about the helicopter?"

"Man of my word."

Ruiz.

"Is this where Catalina and Camila lived?"

"No, Andrés and Valentina's home is on a cliff near the ocean."

"That's right. Catalina's dad is Andrés Ruiz."

Rei squeezed my hand. "It's weird to think that you haven't been out here with the recent weddings."

"Not famiglia." Remembering Dario's apology, I sighed.

"You're my family now, Jasmine. *Mí mamá* will welcome you with open arms."

As we approached the front door of the Ruiz home, it opened. A tired older gentleman greeted us in a bathrobe and slippers. Rei apologized for the hour of our visit.

The gentleman led us through a marble entry and back to glass doors that went out to a pool. The dark sky blanketed the back deck and yard. The only illumination came from the flashing blue-and-red lights on the helipad.

Shit—he was serious.

I wrapped my arms around my midsection, shivering in the cool night breeze. Rei's attention was focused on the blackness above us. It wasn't long before the vibration of a helicopter could be felt as well as heard. Rei placed his hand in the small of my back, pulling me toward his warmth, as a bright spotlight shone down, aimed at the helipad beyond the pool. While the helicopter landed, my hair that Rei had unleashed, blew around my face in the whirling coil from the propellers.

"*Dile al Señor Ruiz gracias,*" Rei said to the gentleman, making his voice louder.

The gentleman waved.

As the rotors continued to spin, Diego opened a door on the side of the helicopter. I hesitated, wondering where I was going. Rei reached for my hand. His warm grasp encapsulated my fingers, sending the spark of his touch through my circulation.

He's your husband.

It was a too-late pep talk, meant to reassure myself that I was where I was supposed to be. I'd told Dario I wanted to marry Rei, and yet in the blink of an eye, I was being whisked away from the only home I'd ever known. A look around the dark yard and at the unfamiliar mansion told me that the man holding my hand was my anchor in this new storm.

I had to trust him.

Beneath the whirling rotors, Rei led us forward. There weren't steps but a high footboard. Soon, the two of us and the pilot were aboard with our luggage. Rei and I were seated in the back seat. I expected some kind of four-point harness, yet our seat belts were like those in a car. Rei handed me a pair of headphones with a microphone, motioning to me to cover my ears.

I placed the headphones over my ears, muffling the thumping of the propellers and held my breath as we were lifted off the ground. The pilot's voice came through the earphones. Like so many other aspects of my new life, I was at a complete loss as to what was said. I looked to my husband for a translation.

"He said the wind is calm. We should reach Bella in less than twenty minutes."

Once the lights of the mainland disappeared, we were surrounded by darkness. The helicopter's dashboard cast an eerie green glow throughout the interior of the cabin. Without the city lights, a million stars sparkled in the sky while below us the Pacific Ocean was a blanket of black.

I gasped as Bella came into view. In a sea of nothingness, blue LED lighting glowed like an aura surrounding the monstrous yacht. The closer we flew, the better I could see what Rei referred to as a big boat. Holy crap. It wasn't a big boat; it was a superyacht. I counted at least four levels, with a swimming pool and hot tub, both glowing with underwater lights. A Mexican flag flew from the rear deck.

"Why the flag?" I asked.

"When Bella is in international waters, as she is now, she is governed by whatever country's flag she flies. Bella is a piece of Mexico in these waters."

I remembered what Camila had said about getting married in Mexico. A peek at my hand told me another wedding wasn't necessary. Rei and I were already married.

"As soon as we land," Rei said, "I will show you to our cabin."

Our.

I turned, taking in his profile. Even in the green hue of the interior lights, Rei was beyond handsome. The ease with which he directed his guards, the man back at the mansion, and the pilot demonstrated his confidence and power.

Would he remember what I said about going slow?
Would it matter?

TWENTY-FOUR

Jasmine

I forgot to breathe as the pilot lowered us to the helipad near the stern of the yacht. Once the landing skids touched down, I took a deep breath.

"We're safe," Rei said.

He sounded a bit annoyed with my fear. That was fine. It was my first helicopter ride over miles of open sea. I had the right to be frightened.

The pilot spoke through the headphones. As before, I couldn't understand. I turned to my husband for a translation.

"He's stopping the rotors. We need to wait until they come to a complete stop. As they slow, they lower. No decapitations on our wedding day"

My eyes opened wide. "Good advice."

As we waited for them to stop, five people in white

uniforms appeared, all standing like soldiers with their hands clasped behind their backs. I looked at my watch to see that it was nearly four in the morning—six back in Kansas City. "This is crazy that the whole staff is meeting us in the middle of the night."

"That's not the whole staff."

Well, shit. My life was on a roller coaster, and I wasn't sure if I wanted to find the exit.

Lingering whirling from the propellers echoed in my ears as one of the men in white came forward and opened the door. As he offered his hand, I glanced at Rei, who nodded. Hesitantly, I took the man's hand and stepped down. My blouse and hair fluttered in the ocean wind.

From our vantage point, I saw into a beautifully illuminated white living room and dining area. Up above, millions of stars shone in the velvet black sky.

This boat was insane, reminding me of news articles I'd read about oligarchs' superyachts. My inadequate acting skills were unable to hide my astonishment. In no way had Rei prepared me for this.

By the time Rei and our luggage were out of the helicopter, another man had joined the greeting committee, causing my nerves to set in. I recognized him from the few times I'd seen him. This was the renowned drug lord himself, Jorge Roríguez.

Rei guided me toward his father.

El Patrón's smile grew as he spread his arms. "Jasmine." His pronunciation was similar to Rei's. "Welcome to Bella."

Wearily, I stepped into his embrace. Spice and cigars

infiltrated my senses as his arms surrounded me. Releasing me from his hug, he said, "Congratulations, *Señora* Roríguez," and patted Rei on the shoulder. "You've made my son a happy man. And that makes Josefina and me happy too."

His accent was thicker than Rei's, but I could still understand his English.

My father-in-law was more gregarious than I anticipated. I hadn't known what to expect. "Thank you for welcoming me." I looked around. "This is truly amazing."

"Tomorrow when you two wake, Rei can give you a tour. There's food waiting for you in your cabin. No rush. You need to rest after your busy day." Jorge then said something to Rei I couldn't understand.

Rei responded with a nod. He returned his hand to the small of my back. "Let me show you to our stateroom."

Our.

My nights of sleeping alone were over.

"What about our luggage?" I asked, looking back toward the helicopter.

"They're probably already in our room."

"You really understated this *big boat*," I emphasized his previous description.

Despite the late or maybe early hour, the common areas of the yacht glowed with golden lighting. I tried to look in every direction at once, but there wasn't time as Rei led me to a staircase. The ocean breeze disappeared as we went down the stairs to a lower deck with multiple doors. "Will I be able to find my way out of here?"

Rei's eyebrows danced. "I don't plan on letting you out of here."

He opened one of the doors, and I couldn't help but open my mouth in awe. Our suitcases were sitting near the bed—a king-sized bed that was already turned down. The sound of the locking mechanism in the door echoed throughout the cabin.

I shuddered as a chill scurried over my flesh. Curiously, I wandered to the far wall. "Are these windows?" I cupped my eyes to see through the opaque pane.

Rei came up beside me, pressed a button, and the glass cleared, revealing a balcony. There was a table with two chairs and two lounge chairs outside.

"That's amazing. I've never seen anything like it."

"It's magic." He scoffed. "Jano and I used to say it was magic when we were young. The sun can be intense out on the ocean. That keeps the sunshine out so we can sleep until noon." He pointed to an armoire. "There's a refrigerator in there with water and juice." He opened the cabinet and removed a crystal decanter with clear liquid. "Tequila?"

I shook my head. "After those margaritas, I may never drink again." Turning a complete circle, I took in the scope of the room, including the mini living room with chairs and a sofa. A basket with fresh fruit was on the coffee table. "This could be our honeymoon."

Rei poured himself some tequila, swirled the liquid, and drank it without so much as a wince. "We're here at *mí padre's* command. With what happened in Culiacán, this is about keeping his family safe."

I sat on the edge of the bed. "Does that include me?"

Rei placed the tumbler on the table, came to me, and crouched near my feet. "*Sí, Señora* Roríguez, that includes you." He slowly and deliberately removed my shoes and socks. "We've had a long day."

My lip was again between my teeth.

Rei stood, taking my hand and encouraging me to follow. Without shoes, my eyes came to the middle of his wide chest, making him seem larger than life or perhaps me, smaller.

His voice lowered an octave. "You want me to go slow?"

I swallowed. "I don't know what I want."

He teased rogue strands of hair away from my face. "You're so fucking beautiful, Jasmine." His intense dark gaze was fixated on me, not allowing me to blink or look away. "When I saw you on the staircase in that gown, I knew that I was about to marry the most stunningly gorgeous woman I'd ever met."

His sandalwood-and-leather scent surrounded us, combined with the aroma of tequila.

Slowly, I lifted my hands to his chest. "I want to get to know you."

It was what he'd said at the lounge.

His lips crashed with mine as he entwined his fingers in my long hair. Our kiss sizzled and sparked, bruising my already-tender lips and stealing my air. As I gasped for breath, his lips moved back to my neck, meticulously kissing from behind my ear to my collarbone and leaving goose bumps in their wake. Closing my eyes, I willed myself to feel the way my body tingled, to get lost in the sensations and the way Rei made my body respond. My head lobbed back, granting him access. His kisses continued to the V of my neckline. I was too lost to realize he was unbuttoning my blouse and kissing lower.

My nipples hardened as he eased my blouse away from my arms.

The heat within me built degree by degree, much as a spark growing to a flame.

Rei fell to his knees and reached for the front of my slacks, unbuttoning and unzipping. The chill of the air conditioning covered my legs with goosebumps as my slacks hit the floor.

Splaying the fingers of his large hand on my lower back with heat radiating from his touch, he steadied me as his mouth lowered. His warm breath hovered over my lace-covered core. As a long, deep hiss filled the air, every nerve in my body was on fire. Like adding fuel to a flame, from the top of my scalp to the tips of my toes, I was ablaze.

TWENTY-FIVE

Jasmine

My knees wobbled as I fought to remain standing.

Rei stood to his feet and scooped me to his chest as if I weighed nothing. My mind was goo as I processed what he'd been doing, where he'd been. It was more intimate than I ever imagined. He laid me on the sheets. For a moment, I considered reaching for the blankets and covering myself. I knew that wouldn't stop whatever Rei had in mind. My thoughts varied wildly from wanting to hide in the bathroom to spreading my legs and taking whatever was coming.

My husband sat on the edge of the bed, his intense stare reading me as if I were an open book. Did he see my fear?

His deep voice ricocheted through me *"Preciosa,* trust me?"

Did I trust him?

Did I have a choice?

Yes, Dario had given me the choice, and I chose Rei.

Inhaling, I nodded.

"I want more of that sweet, warm, wet pussy."

I wondered if all men were so blunt and if I was supposed to be repulsed or turned on. To my own surprise, it was the latter. "How do you know I'm wet?"

Was I actually flirting with my husband?

His lips quirked. "Because I can smell how sweet you are, just as I could smell you the night in the living room."

Scooting up to the headboard, I wanted to tell him he was wrong. That would be a lie.

As Rei stood and began to unbutton his shirt, I was fascinated with the definition of his chest and abs. I'd never seen Rei without a shirt, and it was a sight to behold. If the timeline wasn't wrong, I'd say Michelangelo used Rei as his muse before sculpting the torso of David.

When he turned, his back displayed a tattoo reaching from shoulder to shoulder and down his tapered back. The markings continued down each arm. I suddenly recalled seeing the edge of the artwork from beneath his sleeves the night we went to the Green Lady.

"What is that?" I asked. "Does it have meaning?"

Rei pivoted until his dark gaze met mine. "*Sí,* it's the Roríguez *escudo de armas*—Coat of Arms."

Respect bubbled within me at the pride in his voice. "It's beautiful."

Next, he removed two holsters, laying a gun and a knife on the table. The little dimples at the base of his spine made my core clench. As he bent down to remove his boots and socks, I noticed a plethora of silver scars upon his tanned skin and wondered how he'd gotten them.

Dario had scars I'd noticed on his forearms as did Armando and Piero. Did Rei see them as badges of honor? I didn't want to think about him in harm's way.

When he turned, instead of thinking about that, I concentrated on his wide shoulders and defined arms. My breath caught as he unbuckled his belt, unbuttoned his jeans, and lowered the zipper. His jeans met my slacks on the floor. He then turned back to me wearing nothing but a pair of black boxer briefs.

Oh my God, I could make out his erection beneath the fabric. A million questions came to mind, things I should have asked Camila or Catalina before now. I didn't think Rei would be willing to wait for me to slip into the bathroom and make a frantic call.

"Hey," he said, directing my gaze back to his handsome face. "Talk to me."

I reached for the other pillow and placed it in front of me as if mere material and stuffing could shield me from what was beneath the silk. "I wish I knew what to do. I don't want you to be disappointed in me."

Rei growled and sat on the edge of the bed. "Look at yourself, Jasmine." He tugged the pillow away. "Nothing about you is disappointing." He cupped my cheek. "We will get to know each other." His touch slowly trailed down the familiar path from my cheek to my breasts. "Inch by inch." Shades of brown and black swirled in his dark orbs. "You will tell me what you like and what you don't, if you don't. I plan to make love to you for the next fifty years. I'd like you to want that too."

"Make love?" I blinked. "You said you wanted to fuck me."

"*Sí*, I want both. You said slow. We should start with making love."

I lifted my hand to his warm chest, feeling the frantic drumbeat of his heart. "I've never touched a man."

Rei lifted my hand and kissed the tips of my fingers. "Consider me available to be touched day or night."

He lowered my hand to his erection, pressing it against his rock-hard penis. "Don't be afraid. I won't break either."

Timidly, I rubbed my palm and fingers over the hardness. When my gaze went back to Rei's face, his eyes were closed and his chin raised. His Adam's apple bobbed.

When his eyes opened, they were fixed on me. "My turn."

He reached around my back and masterfully undid my bra before pulling it from my outstretched arms and releasing my breasts.

This was obviously not his first rodeo.

"Fuck," he growled. "Your tits are better than I imagined."

Before I could reply, I gasped as he captured one nipple in his lips and sucked before doing the same to the other. Instantly, my nipples were rock hard. His kisses went lower until they reached the waist of my panties.

"I've wanted to eat your pussy since the first time I smelled your sweet arousal."

How did someone respond to a statement like that?

I didn't have time to come up with the answer before Rei snagged the hem of my panties and to my shock, ripped the lace. "I wanted to do that to the wedding dress."

"You tore them."

Standing, he pulled the ruined material down my legs with a grin. "I did. It's like opening a bag of candy." Grabbing my ankles, he pulled me down before going to the end of the bed and crawling toward me—a lion approaching his prey. "Now spread your sexy legs because I'm ready to eat."

I was about to be his meal.

Trust.

"This is slow?"

Rei laughed, looking up at me with hooded eyes. "*Preciosa*, you're my wife. My hard cock isn't inside your tight pussy. This is slow."

It took a minute, and to Rei's credit he was patient as I finally complied, doing what he asked.

He started near my ankles, kiss by kiss, nip by nip, working his way up. The coarseness of his beard was like the striking of a match on my skin. Higher still, he moved up my legs to my inner thighs. The fire from before was back. The flames raced through my circulation, raising my temperature until his tongue found my folds and a raging wildfire ensued.

I screamed out his name as his tongue delved within me. The stimulation was too much. My legs tried to come together, to stop his assault, but he was too strong. With each buck or wiggle, he held tighter to my legs, pushing them back and away until his face was buried in my core.

The humming within me grew louder, drowning out the primal sounds I was making. My fingers clawed at the sheets, searching for something to ground me. While I knew the premise of what he was doing, I couldn't for the life of me describe the particulars, other than the way it made me feel.

Wound tight as a top ready to spin out of control was a good description.

My uneasiness lapsed into a wanton need as an orgasm hit with the speed of a thundering, out-of-control steam engine. My entire body tensed as the cabin filled with wet, raw noises. I was too far gone to be embarrassed with my inhibition in shreds and my body too weak to move.

Rei climbed up me, depositing kisses as he rose higher until our lips collided. I reached for his head, weaving my fingers through his hair as his tongue tangled with mine, sharing my own taste.

When I finally had the ability to speak, I palmed his cheeks. "No."

Rei lifted an eyebrow. "No?"

"If that's what an orgasm is, when I touched myself, I didn't orgasm."

His lips curled into a smile. "I promise many more."

"You're sure of yourself."

He lowered his forehead to mine. "*Preciosa*, we should sleep."

"But what about you? Do you want me to do something?"

He lifted his face. "Those noises you were making had me ready to come. I loved every syllable and note." He teased my hair away from my face. "I could feel how tense you were."

"I'm not anymore."

"I could sense that too. Tomorrow morning, you'll be less apprehensive." He rolled to my side and pushed his arm behind my back, pulling me to his solid shoulder. After covering us with blankets, he kissed my forehead. "My wife asked for slow. No man ever died from not ejaculating."

That was good to know.

Part of me wanted to protest, to give him a tenth of the pleasure he'd brought me. But honestly, I didn't have the strength. Instead, I curled next to his radiating warmth and closed my eyes.

TWENTY-SIX

Reinaldo

I woke with my arm around someone soft and warm. It took me a second to realize that it was Jasmine within my grasp and in my bed. Her level breathing told me she was still asleep. I leaned toward the side of the bed and reached for my phone.

Fuck, it was after ten in the morning.

I couldn't remember ever sleeping that late. On the other hand, except for a few hours' nap on the plane back to California, prior to falling asleep, I hadn't slept for over forty-eight hours. Maybe I'd need to admit I was human. I needed sleep and food.

My mind went to my bedtime snack.

At first, I was afraid I'd pushed Jasmine too far. It's hard for a man like me to imagine a woman as genuinely naïve as the one I married. With access to Wanderland

and other cartel-owned clubs, my go-to women have mostly been professionals. A long-term relationship with just anyone wasn't something the second son of the drug lord was on the lookout for. I was historically a one-and-done type guy. Even frequenting the same whore too many times gave them the wrong idea.

I knew by Mafia standards, Jasmine was probably a virgin. I knew that for sure when she confirmed it for me that night in her bedroom. A virgin was one thing. Dario Luciano basically raised Jasmine in a convent. Not only was her body pure, but God help us both, so were her thoughts.

Admitting that she'd touched herself was a relief. It gave me hope of her responsiveness.

Last night, I sensed that I was pushing too much and too fast for her to keep up. Of course, I wanted to fuck on my wedding night—didn't everyone?

Nonetheless, I was strangely okay with the way things progressed.

Jasmine and I were getting to know each other.

I may have a reputation as a monster for the way I handle interrogation and the ease with which I take lives, but that didn't extend to the woman I swore to protect and care for. My thoughts went back to just after Jasmine was roofied. She'd asked me if I could love her. I'd said yes for many reasons. One, the capo was standing there. Two, Jasmine was searching for confirmation that she could be loved.

My capacity for love wasn't figured into my answer.

In a world of monsters, love was a weakness—an Achilles' heel.

Staring down at the woman at my side, I marveled at her unique beauty. Her red hair sang to me with a siren's call. I wanted to run my fingers through it, to wrap it around my hand and tighten my grip. One day, Jasmine would not only welcome but want both lovemaking and fucking.

Even if she didn't remember asking, I'd answered her question the right way. I'd risk the weakness to love and be loved by her.

Knowing that she was sleeping completely naked had me harder than a usual morning.

Jasmine's long eyelashes fluttered as she snuggled toward me before her eyes quickly opened and she scooted away.

"Hey," I said, keeping my voice low. "No need to jump. I won't bite." I rolled toward her until our noses nearly touched. "Unless that's something you want."

Her pink lips curled as she blinked away the sleep. Her soft hands came to my cheeks. "I forgot to tell you something last night."

Staring into her eyes was like staring into the deepest depths of the ocean. "What did you forget to tell me?"

A rosy blush filled her cheeks. "I liked what you were doing, what you did."

Bringing my nose to hers, I chuckled. "I mean, you didn't say that, but there were clues." I ran my palm down her back, past her slender waist, and over her firm round ass. "Your skin is so fucking soft."

To my surprise, she pressed her hips toward mine. Only to jump back at finding my contained erection.

"You can be close. I'm not pulling him out until you say so."

Her eyes opened wide. "Me?"

"You."

She supported her head on her hand with her elbow on her pillow. "Why the change? Do you not want me?"

"Fuck, Jasmine. My hard cock should tell you everything you need to know about me wanting you. I also won't force you. I want you to want me."

She laid her head back on the pillow and stared up at the ceiling. "I want you, Rei." She turned to me with wide eyes. "Could I maybe…like you did but me to you?"

"Could you suck me?"

Fuck yes.

"At least touch you," she said.

"Remember, I said I'm always available for touching."

With her lip secured between her teeth, Jasmine sat up, her perfect round tits on full display. Her long veil of red hair flowed over her shoulders as she reached for the blanket and lowered it to my waist.

"*Preciosa*, the blanket can go lower."

Jasmine nodded. "I'll get there."

She'd said anticipation.

"Fuck, I may die first."

Her head moved from side to side as her lips curved. "You said last night that no man has died from not ejaculating."

"It's an untested theory."

She turned, sitting on her knees and stared down at my chest. After an agonizing, indeterminate amount of time, she lowered her hands over my pecs, running her palms over my skin. "How did you get the scars?"

"Knives, mostly." I lifted my arm and showed her a more circular scar. "That one was a bullet."

"I think you need to change your line of work."

"*Mí padre* would disagree."

"I'd rather not think about your father or all the people outside this room right now. They probably know what we're doing."

"Right now, it's not much."

Jasmine's concentration went back to my chest. Her touch moved lower over my abdomen, and she leaned forward, brushing my skin with her lips, whose touch sent shock waves through my entire body, doubling the size of my hardening cock.

She looked up with hooded eyes before kissing my chest again. Her hair skirted over my skin with a ghost of a touch. I had to cross my arms behind my head to stop myself from reaching out. Her sensuous body was so close and yet, I wanted her to go at her own speed.

Jasmine kissed lower until she reached the blanket. Without hesitation, she dragged the blanket down. Her lips followed the dark trail of hair until finally, she snagged the waistband of my boxer briefs and lowered them far enough for my cock to spring free.

I had to bite the inside of my cheek to keep from laughing when she gasped and flinched. With the focus of a surgeon, she studied my penis. The touch of her hands was better than any pharmaceutical enhancement.

Her voice was soft. "It's getting bigger."

"It does that."

Slowly, she leaned forward bringing a kiss to my hardened shaft.

I covered my eyes with one of my arms, certain that instead of a submissive virgin, I'd married a woman well-trained in torture. My body jerked when she licked the tip. "Fuck," I growled, the word resonating from my chest. "Christ."

Peering from beneath my arm, I watched as she tested the water, opening her lips and taking the tip. If she didn't hurry, I was going to come all over her. She fisted me, her fingers and thumb unable to touch and ran her hand up and down my shaft, before once again leaning down and taking me inside her warm mouth.

It took every ounce of restraint not to come with relief.

"Fuck, your mouth feels good."

Her long hair covered her face as she bobbed her head up and down, creating a torturous, agonizing ecstasy. Moans came from her lips as she fidgeted, rubbing her pussy over her heels.

She let out a yelp as my hand landed on her bare ass.

"What was that for?"

My wife was a fucking vision with her swollen lips and drool-covered chin. "You're pleasuring me. You don't get to pleasure yourself at the same time."

"I wasn't."

I lifted an eyebrow.

Her lips curled. "I wasn't sure...but...knowing I'm doing this to you." She shrugged. "It's hot. I'm turned on."

Crooking my finger, I beckoned her to me.

"What?"

"No one brings pleasure to your hot pussy but me. Is that clear?"

Jasmine nodded.

My grin quirked. "I have a solution."

She wiggled toward my chest. "What's your solution?"

"Trust me?"

Jasmine nodded.

"Let me lead."

I directed her until her legs were bent on each side of my head, facing toward the end of the bed. Her weeping pussy was directly over my face. "Now, bend forward."

I was in fucking heaven as we both sucked and licked. The noises were primitive and raw, sloppy and slobbering. As she tensed, my control evaporated. "Fuck, Jasmine. If you don't want to swallow, stop now."

She sat up as if my cock was suddenly on fire.

"Use your hands."

Jasmine did as I said, pumping me dry as my cum oozed over my stomach and her hands. Quickly, she scooted over beside me. "I should have tried to swallow."

Reaching for her shoulders I pulled her over me, my seed a slippery interface. We rolled until I was on top of her. "That was the best fucking blow job, hand job, and sixty-nine of my life."

Her eyes shone as she smiled. "It was all right?"

"Better than all right. Perfection."

Jasmine scrunched her nose. "I should try swallowing."

I ran my thumb over her swollen lips. "You try whatever you want to do."

"Now" —she wiggled beneath me— "I think a shower is in order. I mean, before you present me to your mom, I probably shouldn't have your cum all over me."

"Mine," I whispered. "And now you're marked."

"Yours." Her lips met mine.

TWENTY-SEVEN

Jasmine

Wearing a sundress, sandals, and with my hair pulled back into a low ponytail, I held tightly to Rei's hand, as we entered the dining area a little after noon.

"*Buenos dias,*" Josefina said, sitting on the sofa next to Mia.

"*Buenos dias,*" Rei replied.

Aléjandro came forward. "It's afternoon, Mama. *Buenas tardes.*"

Josefina stood. She was as beautiful as I recalled, with big gold earrings, numerous gold bracelets, and wearing what appeared to be a long black coverup over a bathing suit. Mia on the other hand was reclined, looking uncomfortable as one could nearing her ninth month of a pregnancy. She waved.

Rei walked us closer and spoke to his mother, "I know you've met Jasmine but not as my wife. This is Jasmine Roríguez."

Josefina's smile grew as she came closer and wrapped her arms around me, enveloping me in a cloud of her perfume. "Jasmine, we're sad we weren't able to see Rei wed." Her smile returned. "But now that you're both here, we're happy you did."

"I'm sorry," I said. "Dario wouldn't let me leave without the marriage."

Mia scoffed. "My brother likes to be in control of everything." She pushed herself to stand. With her hands supporting her lower back, she came toward me. To my utter shock, she too spread her arms and wrapped me in an embrace. "I'm glad you convinced him to let you choose your husband."

Had Camila talked to her?

Was she actually on my side?

"Mia," Aléjandro said with a smirk, "didn't get that choice."

Mia pointed to her large midsection. "And look what happened."

"My *nieto* or *nieta* is what is happening," Josefina said with a smile as she laid her hand on Mia's belly.

Mia leaned down to my ear and whispered, "Be warned, if you do more of what you did last night, this is bound to happen to you."

What we did last night?

Could they hear us?

They think we had intercourse.

My gaze went to Rei, but before he could reply, Aléjandro came to Mia's side.

He said, "I think it's a little too late to warn Jasmine away from Roríguez men."

"Now, now," Josefina said, reaching for my hand. "No one gets to frighten Jasmine. Besides" —she gestured with her hand— "we're in paradise." She lowered her voice. "I raised good boys who respect women. If they don't, tell me."

My eyes opened wide. "Rei's been good."

Aléjandro laughed. "That's a solid B- if you ask me."

"Shut the fuck up," Rei said.

"Language," Josefina scolded. Tugging my hand toward the table, she said, "Come, let's get you breakfast or lunch. I want to hear all about the wedding." She looked down at my left hand. "And oh, Rei, these rings are beautiful. Where did you find them?"

As soon as we took seats at the table, a parade of people dressed in white came from what I imagined was the kitchen, carrying pitchers of drinks and trays of food. I'd never seen anything like it. I was used to Contessa, but this was house staff on steroids.

Rei sat beside me with his hand on my thigh as I tried to answer all Josefina's questions. Once *el Patrón* joined us, there were multiple conversations happening as a variety of food filled the table.

"Rei," Josefina asked, "where did you find such lovely rings?"

My gaze went across the table to Mia as my stomach twisted. "Dario had them," I said.

"It's a story," Rei said, "that I think you'd like, Mama."

"It's not—" I tried to interrupt.

Rei went on, "Dario had bought them a long time ago for Jasmine's sister, Josie."

I dared to look across the table. Mia's jaw was clenched, and she had her hand over her midsection. "It's nice," I interjected. "My sister died a few years ago, but now it seems like she's here, approving of my marriage."

Mia stood, pushing back her chair and dropping the napkin on her seat. "I'm sorry." She waved. "I'm not feeling well. I think I need to rest."

"Jano," Josefina said, "will bring a plate of food to your suite."

Exhaling, I looked down.

"Are you all right?" Rei asked.

Fighting tears, I nodded and picked at the food on my plate, no longer hungry.

"Oh, honey," Josefina said. "Mia's close to her time and being out here on the ocean doesn't always settle well."

Aléjandro stood and reached for Mia's plate. "I'll see if she feels like eating."

After he was gone, I turned to Rei and Josefina. "It's okay. Mia hated my sister...and me too." I shook my head and feigned a smile. "It's really all right. I'm used to it."

"The fuck?" Rei said. "Jasmine, that's not true. It might have been, but Mia called me about you. She suggested that I get you out here on Bella to wed." His eyes darkened to nearly black. "She doesn't hate you."

She did call. That was good to know.

Josefina and Jorge exchanged looks.

It was *el Patrón* who spoke, "You're Rei's wife, and you're part of this family. We're happy to have you here. I'm sure it's just pregnancy. I've been told it can be difficult."

"Men," Josefina said. "Can be?"

Looking at Rei, I grinned.

He squeezed my thigh. "After lunch, I'll show you around Bella."

"And later," *el Patrón* said, "you, Jano, and I need to discuss matters."

"Did you bring a bathing suit and sunscreen?" Josefina asked. "The temperatures are cooler here than south, but on the pool deck, it's warm."

"I brought a bathing suit, but I didn't think about sunscreen."

"Oh, I'll have some for you at the pool." She shook her head. "Your beautiful skin would burn. We don't want that."

After lunch, Rei kept his promise, showing me around the multiple decks. Along with the staff dressed in white, there were quite a few men in dark suits. They were hard to miss, especially the one on the lowest deck with the machine gun, or some big gun.

"Guards?" I asked.

"*Sí*, that's where boats dock to bring people aboard. No one gets past that first line of defense who isn't supposed to be here."

It wasn't until we were back in our stateroom that Rei mentioned Mia. "Why didn't you tell me?"

"When have we had the chance to talk, Rei?"

He led me out onto our balcony. We sat at the small table. "Now, we have time."

"No, we don't. Your father wants you and Aléjandro for a meeting. I'm sure that's more important."

He reached across the table and offered me his hand, palm up. Begrudgingly, I laid my hand in his. "Talk to me, *preciosa*."

I shook my head. "It's the same thing, the reason Dario wouldn't allow you to marry me, why he offered Isabella."

"Who the fuck is Isabella anyway? His offer didn't matter. I wanted you."

Swallowing, I tried to keep my composure. "Isabella is Dario's uncle's daughter. She's a Luciano, like Mia."

"You're a Roríguez, like Mia."

My gaze met his as his words computed. "I hadn't thought of that."

"It's the truth. For the record, Mia did call me about you." He inhaled. "She was the one who told me to propose. She called me a pig for me telling you that you're mine."

My cheeks rose in a smile. "I couldn't believe you proposed." I clutched my heart. "You did it in front of everyone."

Rei lowered his head to the table and back up. "What I do for the cartel is dangerous. Knowing my surroundings is cartel 101. In that moment, I didn't even consider who was watching. All I could think about was that you were okay after the roofie and that I wanted to get you out of Kansas City."

"It was beautiful, Rei."

"Better than a B-?"

"An A+" I stood. "I should put on my bathing suit and meet your mother at the pool."

"And I need to go see what is happening. I've been MIA for the last forty-eight hours."

"Should I apologize for that?"

Rei stood and came closer. Snaking his arm around my waist, he pulled my hips to his. "You're here. You're my wife. I've feasted on your delicious pussy and covered us both in my cum. If you think there's anything in that to apologize for, I will have to argue."

My hands landed on his chest. "I don't want to argue with you."

"Then we won't apologize about why I wasn't here." He kissed my forehead. "I'd do it all again to have you here, Jasmine."

"I'm sorry if I'm causing problems with Mia."

"Don't be. *Mí madre* has a way of calming rough waters."

I walked into our suite and looked around. "What happened to our suitcases?" It was then that I noticed the bed was made. A glance in the bathroom told me that our towels were picked up and replaced with clean ones.

"Try the drawers and closet," Rei said. "*Mamá's* staff is thorough."

I opened a drawer to find my underwear. It was in the second drawer that I found my bathing suits. "Oh my God, we are never leaving this boat."

Wearing my bathing suit, I made my way up to the

pool deck. Just before I turned the final corner, Mia came in my direction.

"I'm sorry," I said.

She shook her head. "No, that's on me. Old habits die hard but know I'm doing my best to kill this one. It was hearing her name…"

Josie. My sister.

I nodded. "Now, both of our names are Roríguez."

Mia inhaled. "Well, fuck. You're right."

A smile curled my lips. "What do I need to know about our mother-in-law?"

"Only that she's very intuitive and about the best person you'll ever meet." Mia lowered her voice. "A hell of a lot better than Catalina and Camila's mother-in-law, and I even love my mom."

TWENTY-EIGHT

Reinaldo

"You got Jasmine out of there just in time," Jano said as we walked toward *Padre's* office.

"In time?"

"Myshkin had Kansas City's streets on fire last night."

I stopped dead in my tracks. "What the fuck are you talking about?"

His lips quirked into a smile. "Oh, that's right. You've been out of the loop, too busy popping the ginger's cherry."

My jaw clenched. "Just know, if you weren't my brother, you'd be bleeding out right now. And after what Jasmine told me about Mia, I wouldn't even feel bad making her a widow again."

My brother's cocky grin disappeared. "Sorry about

that. I talked to Mia. It's a long-standing feud, and my wife's more than a little emotional lately. She said she knew it was wrong when she got up from the table and promised to talk to Jasmine."

I shook my head. "I had no fucking clue, but I should have. All the capo's talk about Jasmine not being a Luciano. It makes me want to do whatever I can to make Jasmine feel like we're her family. It's like she's spent her whole life on the edge of luxury, but still outside looking in."

"*Entren aquí*," *Padre* yelled from his office.

Jano and I entered, walking past *Padre's* personal guard.

Wearing his customary white linen shirt, our father sat behind his large desk. "Have you filled him in?" *Padre* asked Jano.

"Haven't had the chance."

"We're spread too thin," *Padre* began. "Our men in México haven't seen Herrera since the attack. Rumor has it that he's not at his compound, but hiding elsewhere, waiting for our next move."

"I say," Jano said, "we give it to him. Blow his fucking place up and let it burn to the ground."

"What happened last night in Kansas City?" I asked.

Padre flattened his lips to a straight line. "There were four coordinated car bombs that went off in Luciano territory beginning at 3:00 a.m."

"After we were gone."

"Salvatore Luciano accused you of coordinating your exit to the bombs."

"The fuck?" I questioned. "I wouldn't do that to the

alliance or the capo and besides, we all know explosives are Myshkin's calling card."

"The capo knows that," *Padre* said. "What they don't know is why the acceleration."

"Herrera," I said, "is running Myshkin's playbook."

Jano sat forward. "The question is where is Herrera? Can we get coordinates on his yacht?"

"You think he's out in these waters?" I asked.

"When Camila was kidnapped," *Padre* said, "the kidnappers were supposed to fly her to Catalina Island. We need satellite coverage of the entire region."

"That's a lot of space," I said. "We're talking off the Latin American and California coasts. Fuck, that's nearly thirty-two hundred kilometers or two thousand miles. And his yacht isn't as big as this one. It would be like looking for a needle in a haystack."

Jano had his phone out, his fingers flying over the screen. "I just told Nick to see what he can find. The government has the technology. We just need to hack into their system."

"What if Herrera is hiding out with Myshkin and encouraging him to accelerate the attacks on the famiglia?" I asked.

Padre leaned back in his chair. "It would be like shooting ducks in a bucket if we could get the two of them together."

My cheeks twitched as I tried not to laugh. *Mí padre* botched up the saying: shooting fish in a barrel.

"We need to send our best men," Jano said, "to Kansas City and get confirmation of Herrera."

Padre leaned forward and put his elbows on the top of his desk. "I'm looking at our best men."

"I'm not leaving Mia," Jano said, looking at me.

"I just fucking got married yesterday."

"The women will be safe on Bella." He looked at Jano. "Mia's not due for what...a month."

"Babies don't necessarily follow schedules," Jano replied. "With Mia being thirty, the doctor said the baby could come early or late."

"I don't follow schedules either," Padre said. "You'll both go today. When you return, I want either the confirmation of Myshkin's and Herrera's location or their blood on your hands."

Jano's nostrils flared as his gaze met mine. There was no getting out of this mandate.

Ten minutes later, I was with Jasmine in our stateroom, me dressed for battle and my wife in a sexy black bikini.

"You're leaving?" she asked with fresh tears in her eyes.

I reached for the floppy hat covering her gorgeous hair and pulled it from her head. "I'll be back. I promise. You'll be safe here with my parents and Mia."

"Mia."

Snaking my arm around her trim waist, I pulled her hips against mine. "Jano said she felt bad about leaving the table."

Jasmine shook her head. "I'm not worried about Mia. We'll learn to navigate this." She looked down at how our bodies were pressed together and back up. "Rei, you promised we'd get to know one another. I expect you to keep that promise."

This was fucking difficult.

I lowered my lips to her forehead, the aroma of sunscreen filling my senses before I kissed her soft skin. "I'm a man of my word." My lips quirked. "And while I'm gone, you have permission to pleasure yourself, as long as you're thinking about me."

"It isn't the same."

I lifted my brow. "Good."

"I've never come like I did last night or this morning. I can't do that alone."

"Your choice, *preciosa*. When I return, I want you ready to take me, all of me. Fucking or making love is your choice."

She nodded. "I'll never stop thinking about you."

I cupped her cheek. "Fuck, Jasmine. This is what I do. When *mí padre* says jump, we fucking jump. If he thought other men could do what Jano and I can do, he'd send them. We're fucking good at this."

"I understand." She reached for my arm, the one with the bullet scar, and lowered her lips to the circular reminder. "Don't get shot."

"I'll do my best."

"Will you at least call me?"

"I'll try. It will depend on if we can without calling attention to ourselves."

"Are you going to fly inland on the helicopter?"

"No, we'll take a boat. Again, less spotlight. Boats come and go from San Diego's ports."

"Down to where the man with the machine gun is?"

I nodded. "Come with me?"

With my duffel bag over my shoulder, we quietly walked hand in hand through the passageways and down the stairs until we made our way down to the boat ramp. Jano and Mia were there when we arrived. It was obvious by her swollen eyes that Mia had been crying.

I squeezed Jasmine's hand.

Joaquín, one of *Padre's* guards and boat captain, pulled a forty-eight-foot cigarette boat up to the floating platform. After I left Jasmine with one more kiss, Jano and I stepped from the deck to the platform and down into the boat.

"Mia isn't taking this well," I said as we both took seats.

"I'm not fucking either. Let's get this shit done. I want to see my son come into this world."

As Joaquín accelerated the boat, my eyes widened. I slapped Jano on the shoulder. "A boy. Fuck, congratulations."

He looked at me as if he was shocked I knew the information he'd just shared. "Don't you dare tell Mia you know. That goes for Jasmine too."

"Won't say a word. A little Reinaldo."

"No way am I telling you his name. You're going to wait like everyone else."

Diego and Felipe met us at the docks and drove with us back to the airport. As the cartel's Gulfstream came into view, I shook my head. "I was just on this plane and now I'm back."

The four of us boarded the plane. After a brief talk with the pilot and attendant, we started working. I had my computer in front of me as did Jano. Felipe and Diego were coordinating with the famiglia guards through their tablets.

We hadn't landed in Kansas City yet when Nick sent us the geocode coordinates of four yachts possibly belonging to Elizondro Herrera. "We need to send boats out to surveil these yachts. If we get license numbers, we'll have a better idea if Herrera owns them."

"The ownership would be buried under layers of LLCs," I said. "It's not like it will have Elizondro Herrera on it."

"No shit," Jano replied. "Check the file I just sent you. It contains sixty-eight LLCs we've connected to Herrera."

"When did you get this?"

"Been working on it while you've been running around like a lovesick puppy."

I wasn't fucking apologizing. Opening the file, I scanned the spreadsheet. "Good work. What if we reverse search to see if any of these LLCs can be associated with Myshkin?"

Jano nodded.

Padre was right. We worked well as a team.

TWENTY-NINE

Jasmine

When I entered the dining room for breakfast, the somber mood was palpable. I took the seat across from Mia, Josefina to my side at one end where she always sat.

"Any word?" I asked, pulling out my chair.

Mia shook her head.

It had been three days since we'd said goodbye to our husbands on the boat ramp. Three days since we stood next to one another and watched the long cigarette boat soar out of sight.

Immediately, members of the staff were present, filling my coffee cup and serving me fresh fruit.

"Your omelet, *Señora*, will be a few minutes."

"No, thank you," I said. "Maybe just an English muffin."

When the staff member walked away, Josefina reached toward me. "Jasmïne, not eating won't bring Rei back any sooner. I don't want him upset with me if you lose weight."

"I'm really not hungry, and I don't want to waste your food."

"It is our food. You need protein."

Mia watched our conversation with an amused expression. "Jasmine, you might as well give in. I promise you won't win. Especially if Josefina thinks there's a remote chance you could be pregnant."

"There's not."

Josefina opened her big brown eyes wider. "There's always a chance. You need to take care of yourself."

"I'm pretty sure you have to actually have intercourse to get pregnant."

"You're married," she replied.

Lifting my napkin from my lap, I laid it on the table. "I'm not entirely comfortable with this conversation."

"Jasmine," Mia said, "stay and eat." She turned to Josefina. "Jano and I didn't have intercourse for almost a week after we were married." She smiled at me. "If Rei is anything like his brother, they're good men who respect their wives. I think that's where this conversation should center."

I sighed with relief. "We are only now getting to know one another."

Josefina leaned back as the server brought my English muffin. "*Ella tambiïn comerá tocino.*"

The server nodded and walked away.

"I'm getting more food?"

Our mother-in-law smiled. "*Sí*. You are too thin."

I didn't think I was too thin. If anything, I thought I could stand to lose a few pounds.

"See, I told you," Mia said with a grin. She turned to Josefina. "Where's Jorge?"

She shook her head. "In his office. All he tells me is that the boys are safe. But I know my husband, he's stressed." She glanced between the two of us. "Not for the boys."

Boys.

I was pretty sure Reinaldo and Aléjandro were men—I knew it.

"About Herrera," she went on. "I heard him speaking to Silas. When they find him, it won't be good." She inhaled and pressed her lips together as a plate with five pieces of bacon was delivered to me. "Protein."

"Speaking of Silas..." Mia said. Directing her speech toward me, she added, "Silas is the head of Jano's and my security. He and his wife Viviana used to work in Mexico for Jorge and Josefina." She turned to Josefina. "My mother wants to visit. I'm afraid she's not willing to wait until my due date. Has Silas given you any idea when I can tell her we'll be back to the mainland?"

Josefina feigned a smile. "Arianna is welcome on Bella."

Mia met my gaze and shook her head.

A truce of sorts had been worked out between Mia and me. Arianna Luciano would be a whole other level of problem. I wasn't certain I'd ever heard her speak my name.

Mia continued, "I don't think having Mom on Bella will work, but she can stay with Silas and Viviana until I return." She ran her hand over her midsection. "Jano joked about having an obstetrician on Bella. If he doesn't get back with good news soon, that may be what we need."

"Are you feeling anything?"

"Just very large."

A few hours later, I was lying near the pool, fully sunscreened and wearing a big floppy hat, both worn at the persistence of my mother-in-law when she took the lounge chair at my side.

"Did I mention that I have shelves of books in my office. You're welcome to borrow one." She pulled a book from her bag. I couldn't read the title. Before I could ask, she added, "Don't worry. I have many in English as well."

"Rei showed me your office, but I can't remember where it was, and I'm trying not to wander."

"On the first level. Child, you're welcome to wander. This is now my home and you're family." She scrunched her nose. "The only place to avoid is Jorge's office. I don't go there unless invited."

"Thank you for making me feel welcome." I laid my head back against the chair and closed my eyes. "This isn't the way I imagined spending my first days as a married woman."

Josefina sat up and put her feet on the ground toward me. "It occurred to me that you were raised by your sister?"

I nodded. "Pretty much all I can remember."

"And she's gone?"

My heart ached. "She was killed a few years ago."

Josefina reached over to my arm. "My favorite job in this world is being a mother. Jano and Rei are my life. I'm not trying to take Catalina's place, but being away from home can be difficult. If you ever want to have someone to talk to, you can always talk to me."

"Thank you. Catalina is more of a friend." I sighed. "The thing is, I have a mother."

"You do?"

"*El Patrón* must not have told you because Rei said Jorge knew. My mother was incarcerated when I was very young. Just before leaving Kansas City, I learned that she is out on parole."

"Do you want to see her?"

I shrugged. "I can't answer that. Josie, my sister, never spoke about her. Dario doesn't have a high opinion. I tried to get ahold of her before Rei proposed, but I haven't heard anything from her."

When I sat up, I realized Mia was seated at an umbrella table behind us.

"Sorry for eavesdropping," she said. "I didn't know your mom was out of prison."

"Yeah, another reason to not like me."

Mia came forward and stood by our chairs. "I have a better reason for you to never forgive me."

Twisting my legs to the side of the lounge chair, I faced Josefina and turned to Mia. "Why?"

"Rocco is the one who killed Josie." Distress showed in Mia's expression. "I've known that since it happened. I never told Dario. I probably shouldn't be telling you."

My breath caught. "Your husband…why?"

"My *dead* husband, may he rot in hell. He was ordered to do it." She tilted her head. "Just like Jano and Rei follow orders, Rocco did too. Hell, he wasn't smart enough to come up with the shit on his own. There was nothing he wouldn't do to grovel and prove his fidelity to my father. Murder wasn't even his worst sin."

"Your father put out the hit on my sister?" I asked incredulously.

"I also think that Rocco was the one who scared you before classes started your freshman year in New York." She exhaled. "He didn't tell me that. I put the pieces together when Catalina told me what happened to you. Rocco had been out of town for a couple of days and when he came back, his arm was bandaged."

I nodded. "I knew that. Piero shot the intruder in the arm. When Rocco came to the apartment with his arm bandaged, Catalina and I realized he was the intruder."

"I'm sorry, Jasmine. Part of the reason I've avoided you was that since Josie's death, I felt guilty."

"We need to tell Dario," I said.

"Rocco is dead. I don't think there is any more punishment possible."

"But still, he should know the truth."

"That's up to you. At least now you know the truth."

My gaze briefly met Josefina's before I took a deep breath, stood, and walked a few steps to where Mia was standing. "Thank you for telling me. We knew she was targeted but thought it might have been the bratva."

"That's what you were supposed to think."

I looked into her hazel stare. "Maybe we can try to start over, as Roríguez wives."

Mia shook her head. "You should hate me."

"I've done that already. It's time for something new." I had a thought. "Does Mrs. Luciano know about Rocco and Josie?"

"I don't think so. The only person I've ever talked to about it was Rocco and now you."

Josefina stood and wrapped her arms around both of our shoulders. "God, he works in mysterious ways. This is good for the two of you." Her hands came down clutching our hands. "My daughters, you're now sisters."

I squeezed her hand back. "I think I'm going to try to find your office. Fiction sounds like a nice escape." Although I initially headed for the stairs to the first level, I sidetracked and made my way to Rei's and my stateroom. By the time I found my phone, my hands were shaking.

Swiping my contact list, I hit Dario's contact. My diamond ring caught my attention. "I'm so sorry, Josie," I said aloud as Dario's phone rang in my ear. After the beep, I hesitated. This wasn't something I wanted to leave on his voicemail.

As I hung up, I received a text message. Praying it was from Rei, I went to my messages. Disappointment washed over me at the unknown number. I clicked on the message.

· · ·

"*Jasmine, this is your mother. I'd like to talk to you as soon as you feel comfortable. I've missed knowing about your life. Maybe you can make a little room for me, now that you're married. To reach me, follow this link.*"

Something felt wrong.

How does she know I am married?

THIRTY

Reinaldo

The fucking car smelled like fast-food and body odor. It wasn't a good combination. I tried to remember Jasmine's honeysuckle scent as I stared through the windshield of the inconspicuous sedan. This was the fifth night of surveillance outside Myshkin's club in the bratva territory. At nearly two in the morning, we were no closer to going back to Bella than we'd been when we stepped off the fucking boat deck.

"I need to piss," Diego said, opening the car door.

Laying my head against the seat, I dreamed of less time undercover and more time under the covers with my wife.

I would call Jasmine if I could. Jano worried about our phones being tracked. So, they're now locked in a lead-lined box at the capo's place. The box was specifically designed to block phone signals. Instead, I was carrying a cheap burner that connected me to Jano, Felipe, Diego, and the members of the Luciano famiglia involved in our operation.

We'd been on the lookout for Kostya Myshkin and Herrera. The only ranking person we'd seen in the last four days was Zhdan Myshkin. As much as I'd like to put a cap into his brain, he wasn't our main concern. The arrogant son of a bitch was the one who roofied my wife. Before I left Kansas City, I might make his killing an extracurricular activity.

Taking a sip of my Coca-Cola, I wished for a Tropicola. Unfortunately, the fast-food restaurants in Kansas City didn't carry the Cuban-made soda. Coke was about as close as I could get. When this was over, I'd fucking bathe in tequila.

As Diego got back into the car, my cheap phone vibrated. I answered the call. *"Hola."*

Jano's voice came through loud and clear. "A message came through from Em, not sure when it was sent. The drone made a hit on the yacht Nick found off of Bahía Asunción."

"Bahía Asunción—Mexican jurisdiction," I said with a grin.

"Sí. Easier to sweep away."

"It would cost some money, but that was an easier route than dealing with the Coast Guard or FBI. Fuck," I said. "Do we know for sure Herrera was on it?"

"Not for sure. Confirmed his wife and kids were. No one got off. Fucker's probably still burning as we speak."

"Fuck."

Jano hummed in agreement. "Three kids, I think."

"If Elizondro wasn't on that boat, he's retaliating."

"Our *padre* is aware. Bella is equipped with high-definition cameras, acoustic sensors, RF sensors, and radar. Nothing is getting near her without warning."

"Does the capo know?" I asked.

"Not yet. He's my next call." Jano was on a different street watching other doors to the club. "Any action on your side?"

"No. Boring as shit."

"Call the capo," I said. "I'll keep watching the private entrance." Blinking, I leaned forward. "Shit, people are coming out." The person passed within a circle of illumination. I tapped Diego's arm. "Fucking bingo."

"Myshkin?" Jano asked.

My tone was deadly calm. "Both of them with two goons flanking them. I'm hanging up. Get the fuck out of here. This place is about to be swarming with Russians." I hit the red button and placed the phone in my pocket as Diego opened our weapon box in the back seat.

Our long-range rifles were the best money could buy. With the attached magazine, we could fire off ten rounds. Two to three rounds per second, and we'd be long gone before anyone could identify us. Diego and I didn't need the red dot sights the Russians used when they invaded the Ruiz home.

Hell no.

We were both deadly accurate from 500 yards or less.

If I were to guess, the men we were watching had just received word of Herrera's yacht. They were all talking about something they deemed important, too important to thoroughly assess their surroundings.

Without a word, Diego and I waited as they made their way toward a car parked behind the Russian club. My heart beat steadily in my chest as the rush of adrenaline filled my veins. I tapped my finger on the console as a countdown.

As soon as I tapped the third tap, we opened our doors and began shooting. Even Myshkin's guards didn't have time to react. Within seven seconds, we were back inside the car, and I had the motor running. I tossed my phone to Diego. "Call Jano. Tell him it's done. We'll meet at the capo's. If this doesn't bring Herrera out of hiding, I don't know what will."

"Unless he's already dead," Diego said.

"That would be the best news."

Armando, one of the capo's guards met us in the garage. "You can go to Mr. Luciano's to clean up before going up to the penthouse."

For a second, I looked at Jano, Diego, and Felipe, before surveying myself. Five days with little sleep and less hygiene had taken their toll. "That's a good plan."

After a hot shower and clean clothes, I walked out into Dante's living room to find Camila sitting on the sofa. "Did I wake you?"

She shook her head. "How's married life?"

"I'm fucking hoping I can fly back west tonight and find out."

"I'm not sure what's been going on, but to say it's been tense around here is an understatement."

I sighed. "You better ask your husband about that."

"I would, but he left a few hours ago for San Diego."

I stood straighter. "Why?"

Camila's green eyes opened wide. "I was hoping you knew."

"I need to get upstairs and talk to the capo."

Camila nodded. "I have my card. I'll take you up."

When the elevator doors closed, Camila smiled. "Tell Jasmine I miss having her around."

"Will do," I replied with a nod.

The doors opened to the capo's entryway. Armando stood guard outside of Dario's office. As I approached, I heard my brother's voice.

"...fuck weren't we informed?"

"You had a job to do. You did it."

I turned the corner as Jano's voice got louder. "We should have been called."

"And then Myshkin would still be a threat."

Entering, I saw the capo standing on the other side of the desk. His suit coat and tie were gone. My brother's hair was still wet, and he had on fresh clothes. Our phones lay on the capo's desk.

Jano's dark stare met mine. "Fuck."

"*Qué pasa?*" I turned to the capo.

"We're still trying to figure out what happened," he said. "Dante landed about an hour ago."

"Landed where? What are you talking about?"

What had Camila said—Dante was in San Diego?

Jano gripped my arm. "Bella."

A death grip came to my heart and my circulation ceased to flow. "What about Bella?"

It was the capo who spoke. "The yacht was hijacked

just after sunset last night. From what we've learned through the distress call, a boat with five Russians from Kozlov's bratva boarded Bella, took out the first sentry." He shook his head. "There was a gun battle. Two of the Russians were killed."

"Two Russians. What about *Padre's* guards?"

Jano shrugged and shook his head. "We don't have answers."

My mind did the math on the timing. Sunset was close to 7:00 p.m. That would be 9:00 p.m. in Kansas City. It was now three in the morning. "Six hours." Placing my hand on my head, I pulled my wet hair. "What the fuck? Where's Jasmine? Where's Mia?" I looked at Jano. "Our parents."

My brother's jaw clenched. "They're looking for the yacht."

THIRTY-ONE

Jasmine
Seven hours ago

Aléjandro and Mia's stateroom was next door to ours. I hadn't determined if they could have heard Rei and me through the walls, but I didn't doubt it was a possibility. Since Rei left, there wasn't anything to hear except music or a podcast.

During a few of my late-night sleepless hours, I'd tried unsuccessfully to recreate the orgasms Rei had wrung from me. I tried pretending they were his fingers and not mine. I even imagined his tongue and whatever he did with his teeth. My imagination could get me wound up, but the coming down was anti-climactic in all senses of the term.

It seemed impossible to be bored on a superyacht, but I was. I'd completed all the assignments for my classes, read two books, and spent more time than ever in my life resting in the sun. I was a newlywed and what I really wanted was time with my husband.

With dinner not being served until eight at night, I was showered and dressed, with over an hour to kill. Going out onto the balcony, I stood at the railing and stared out at the ocean. The horizon created a darker blue line separating the water from the sky. It truly was beautiful and far different than the view from my room in Kansas City.

My skin prickled at the sound of someone yelling.

Who would be yelling?

I took a step closer to the wall separating our balcony from Jano and Mia's.

"Oh shit." Am I hearing Mia?

Running through the stateroom, I opened my door and gripped the doorknob of the room next door. It was locked. "Mia," I called through the door. "Mia."

Back in our stateroom, I found my phone, thankful that we'd exchanged numbers. Calling Mia, I bit my lip, hoping I was wrong. She'd answer and say she was fine. Maybe she was watching a loud movie.

The call went to voicemail. I ran back out on the balcony, where I'd first heard it and called her name. "Mia." I paused. "Mia," I screamed louder. "Are you all right?"

"Jasmine."

I could barely hear her.

"Get Josefina. I'm bleeding."

One of the few places I hadn't been on Bella was to Jorge and Josefina's private quarters. I also knew that

Josefina enjoyed resting before dinner. As I passed one of the staff members, I asked, "Do you have keys to get into the staterooms?"

"*Sí*, are you locked out, *Señora*?"

"No, I think Mia—*Señora* Mia Roríguez—is in trouble. We need to get into her room. Please. She's bleeding."

The woman's eyes widened. "*Señora* Roríguez—Josefina."

"I'm on my way to get her."

The woman hurried toward Mia's cabin. Two large doors marked the entrance to Josefina's quarters. I pounded on the door and called her name. "Josefina." My fist ached as I pounded.

The door opened inward. Josefina was standing before me in a bathrobe. "I'm sorry to bother you."

Alarm showed in her eyes. "Is everything okay?"

Jorge came from behind her, looking as discombobulated as I'd ever seen him. There wasn't time to think about what I'd interrupted. I concentrated on Josefina. "No." I shook my head. "It's Mia. I couldn't get to her, but I heard her..."

"Mia." She turned around saying something I couldn't understand to her husband before rushing past me. "We need to get to her. It's too early for the baby."

"She said she was bleeding."

I ran beside Josefina as she took the quickest route to Mia's room. As we approached the door was open. Our steps slowed and Josefina entered before me. Mia was lying on the bathroom floor covered by towels. A member of the staff was with her, using a stethoscope to listen for the baby's heartbeat. Mia looked up at us with a tear-stained face and puffy eyes.

The staff member spoke in Spanish. While I didn't understand him, Mia and Josefina did, as they both took long, ragged breaths. Josefina hurried to Mia. "We need to get you to a hospital. I don't care what Jorge says."

Mia nodded. Her gaze came to mine. "You heard me."

"I did. I'm sorry I didn't hear you sooner."

With our help, Mia dressed. She said she'd been in the shower when she felt the cramping and saw the blood. When she got out, she doesn't know if she passed out or what happened. She woke on the floor, afraid to move, and started to call for help.

"Get your purse, ID, and phone," Josefina said to me.

"Why? Where am I going?"

"With me. You're an American citizen. I have fake identification, but I don't want trouble."

The dots became connected. "We're going with Mia?"

"*Sí.* Jorge wants us to take guards with us. He's calling Silas to meet Mia at the helipad."

"We're flying?"

She shook her head. "We won't all fit in the helicopter, and Mia can't ride in a boat across choppy water. She'll need to fly with guards. You, I, and more guards will travel by boat."

"Is there any way to contact Aléjandro?" I asked.

Josefina's expression grew solemn. "Jorge says no."

I reached for her hand. "Are our husbands alive?"

"*Sí,* Jorge swears it."

"Is he coming?"

"No. Something horrible happened today. If he's found in the States, they will arrest him."

"What happened?"

Josefina's posture straightened. "Not our business. Right now, Mia is our concern and in our prayers."

I watched as Mia was carried to the helicopter and strapped into the back seat. Two of the dark-suited men also boarded with the pilot. One sat in the co-pilot's seat and the other sat next to Mia. As the helicopter took off, blowing my dress and hair, I looked around, taking in the lack of guards.

"Come," Josefina called. "Joaquín, the boat captain, is almost here."

Following my mother-in-law down multiple sets of stairs, we came to the boat deck. The guards I'd been looking for were here. A long thin boat was being moored to the deck. Once it was secure, the captain offered his hand, helping Josefina and I into the boat. As soon as we were seated, two more men in dark suits joined us. Josefina secured a scarf over her long hair. I shivered from the ocean breeze as I huddled near Josefina. "I should have brought a coat."

The captain opened one of the seats and removed a blanket. "*Señora*," he said, handing it to me.

"*Gracias*." I had enough time to wrap the blanket around me before the boat was untied and sped away from the setting sun.

Leaning closer, I spoke to Josefina. "We took four of the guards. Will Jorge be okay?"

She nodded, but I could see the concern in the lines around her brown eyes. I reached out and took her hand.

"Mia and the baby will be all right. Didn't she say she was thirty-six weeks?"

Josefina nodded. "We can pray."

It wasn't until the lights of the mainland came into view that I finally relaxed—if that was even possible. I kept telling myself that this boat was how Rei and Aléjandro traveled. *El Patrón* wouldn't allow Josefina to travel this way if it wasn't safe.

One of the guards turned and spoke to Josefina after reading a text message. Once he was finished talking, I looked at my mother-in-law.

"Mia is now with Silas and Viviana. They're on their way to the hospital, and they've called Mia's doctor."

I missed Piero. In the sea of dark-suited men surrounding us, I wasn't confident as to who I could trust. I stayed close to Josefina as we were transferred from the long boat to a waiting SUV. The sun was fully set by the time we arrived at the hospital. The guard who had given us the news about Mia must also be informed as to her current whereabouts. When the other man pulled the SUV up to the hospital, the second guard got out and opened our door. Without a word, we followed him around the metal detectors.

I kept expecting someone to tell us we couldn't walk around them, but we needed to walk through them. No one stopped us. He then led us to elevators that took us up to the fifth floor and to a secure door. He spoke to the speaker in Spanish and the door opened.

Once we passed a nurse's station, we were directed down a private hallway. There was a dark-suited man outside the door who simply nodded as Josefina and I made our way into the room.

An older couple was standing by Mia's bed.

Josefina rushed to Mia's side. My sister-in-law was wearing a medical gown and lying on a bed. There was a big belt around her midsection and multiple screens with numbers and graphs. She already had an IV in her arm.

The older woman came my direction. "You must be Jasmine."

"I am."

She smiled. "I'm Viviana, Silas's" —she motioned to the man— "wife. We hear you're the one who heard Mia calling for help. We're so thankful you saved her."

"I didn't save her, but I heard her. What have the doctors said?" I asked.

Mia nodded toward the screens. "See that second one on the right? It's monitoring the baby's heart rate."

I stepped closer and read the monitor. "One hundred and fifty? Isn't that high?"

Mia shook her head. "It's strong, where it's supposed to be. They've done an ultrasound. If they can stop labor they will, if not" —tears filled her eyes— "we're having a baby."

"Oh, honey," Josefina said. "Jano will be here soon. I know it."

I wanted to ask if she truly knew about Aléjandro or if she was being positive. As a sense of dread sent a chill over my flesh, I feared it was the second.

The hospital room had a couch, a table with two chairs, and a recliner. As Mia napped, Josefina and

Viviana chatted quietly on the couch. Silas sat at the table, and I sat in the recliner. The food the guards brought us wasn't even close to edible when compared to the meals Josefina's staff had been feeding us on Bella.

I wasn't sure how I did it with the nurses and aides coming in and out of Mia's room, but somehow, I must have fallen asleep. I woke with a gasp, noticing I'd been covered with a blanket and the sky was still dark through the windows. Dante was standing against a wall. However, none of that mattered as much as the vision of two large men entering the hospital room.

Aléjandro rushed to Mia's side.

Springing from the recliner I closed my eyes as Rei's strong arms surrounded me.

"Preciosa."

THIRTY-TWO

Reinaldo

Burying my nose in Jasmine's hair and inhaling her honeysuckle scent calmed the raging beast within me. It was as if I could physically feel my blood pressure dropping to a healthy reading. Her arms wrapped around my torso as she laid her face against my chest. It took a moment for me to realize she was crying. Loosening my grip, I palmed her cheeks and tilted her face toward mine. "Why are you crying?"

She blinked, her blue eyes staring up at me. "I've been so scared. I was afraid something terrible happened." She shook her head. "It was a feeling I couldn't shake."

"*Sí*, something did." Ignoring the others in the room, I turned to *mi madre*. "Jano and I need to talk to you."

"If this is about Herrera's yacht, *su padre* already told me."

My brother inhaled. "There's more."

Madre visibly paled as she sat on the sofa and reached for Viviana's hand. Her lips began to tremble. "Not *su padre*." She shook her head. "No. No. No." Each word was louder than the one before.

Jano and I went to her, both of us on our knees near her legs. "Bella was attacked tonight," I said in the calmest voice I could muster. "Herrera had Volkov send a team of men in response to the bombing of his yacht."

"No," she wailed. "It's not true."

"One of the crew was able to send a distress call," Jano said, his voice as flat as mine. "The Coast Guard found Bella approximately fifty miles west of where it had been." Jano reached for her hand. "There's no way to say this to make it better. He's gone. The staff" —his nostrils flared— "all of them—executed."

Madre leaned forward and clung to both of us. For what seemed like an eternity, the only sound I could hear was that of my mother's sobbing. And then I realized she wasn't the only one. When I stood, I searched for my wife.

Jasmine was sitting on the side of Mia's bed, the two embracing and crying.

Jano and I had done our share of shouting and yes, even crying. We had an over three-hour flight to work out our sorrow. Now our focus was on revenge.

Silas had left a message on Jano's phone about Mia. That voicemail was our solace as we headed west. Losing

Papá was heartbreaking. If we'd lost everyone, we would have burnt the world down until there was nothing left but a smoldering pile of ash.

Once in the air, Jano contacted Silas and told him to keep all news away from the women. When it came to delivering such heart-wrenching information, it was better for it to come from us rather than hearing from a talking head on television.

The news outlets were filling the airways, podcasts, and social media with sensationalized stories about drug lords Elizondro Herrera and Jorge Roríguez and their deadly feud. Pictures of Herrera's young family showed in a split screen with his burning yacht. The anchors and podcasters made *Padre* out to be a monster, a criminal solely responsible for every illegal drug-related death in the Americas. Our *madre* didn't need to see or hear that.

"What happens now. Will there be a funeral?" Jasmine asked when we were alone in the hospital cafeteria.

I shook my head. "No. It would be a target, and Jano isn't going to allow that."

"I'm sorry. I was scared to meet your father, but he was nothing but nice to me." A tear streamed down her cheek. "He was so excited about a grandchild."

Wiping her cheek with my thumb, I caressed her soft skin. "Death is part of life. We all know the risks we take."

Jasmine shook her head. "I don't want you to die."

My lips quirked. "I don't plan on it. Not anytime soon."

"What will happen to Bella?"

"She's been seized. The government will take her and sell her." I clenched my jaw. "They'll claim they're selling her for unpaid tax debts, but in truth, they're doing it to make a mockery out of *mi padre's* life." I reached over to Jasmine, holding her hands in mine. "When we first heard, Jano and I" —my nostrils flared— "you, Mia, *Madre...*" I blinked away salty tears *mi padre* would never want me to shed. "It's a miracle you weren't on Bella."

"What about all of us? Will the government come after you and Aléjandro?"

"We'll need to lie low, but soon, we will be up and running. Only now, Jano is in charge of everything."

"What about your mother?"

Forcing a smile, I said, "*Preciosa*, you haven't seen our home yet, but it's big."

Jasmine grinned. "Like Bella is a big boat?"

"*Sí*. It's very big. How do you feel about *mí madre* staying with us? I know that's not what every new bride wants to hear."

She squeezed my hands. "I think I'd love that. Do you know what today is?"

"The day we will meet our nephew?"

Jasmine's eyes widened. "A boy? They're having a boy."

"Shh." I laid my finger over her lips. "We don't know that and if you say anything, Jano will never trust me again."

"How long have you known?"

"Just since we left for Kansas City."

Jasmine reached for her cup of coffee. "How did things go in Kansas City?"

"We took out Myshkin—both of them—so you will never need to be scared of Zhdan again and the connection with Myshkin and Herrera is broken for good." I nodded. "We accomplished our goal."

"Good." Jasmine reached for her phone. "I should tell you that I received a text message from my mother."

My brow furrowed as I took her phone and read the message. It was dated two days ago.

"JASMINE, *this is your mother. I'd like to talk to you as soon as you feel comfortable. I've missed knowing about your life. Maybe you can make a little room for me, now that you're married. To reach me, follow this link.*"

"DID YOU CLICK THE LINK?" I asked.

Her bottom lip disappeared between her teeth. "I didn't. Something felt off. For one thing, how would she know we were married? It wasn't like Dario had it published in the newspaper."

"We filed a marriage license."

"Again, why would she be informed?"

"Myshkin knew," I said, thinking about the problems he caused in Kansas City the night we wed. "Your mother is definitely connected to Myshkin."

Jasmine exhaled.

"We helped the famiglia out with their problem. Now they're going to help us out with ours."

"Is that why Dante is here?"

I nodded.

"You didn't answer my question about today."

"It's our one-week anniversary."

CHAPTER

THIRTY-THREE

Jasmine
Four days later

We'd spent the last few nights at Aléjandro and Mia's house. Now, with Arianna on her way from Kansas City to meet her grandson, Jorge, it was time for us to move up to Sacramento. We had no way of knowing if Jorge had been the planned name all along, but the way Josefina's face lit up when she first held the perfect seven-pound, thirteen-ounce bundle of joy confirmed that it was the perfect name.

The first night in our home, just as I settled under the covers of our bed and began reading a new book, the door to our bedroom opened inward, and Rei entered, looking tired and oh so handsome.

"How is your mom doing?" I asked.

"She's settled. I think she wanted to stay with baby Jorge longer."

"She'll have more chances after Mrs. Luciano leaves."

Rei began to remove his shirt. "*Madre* has an entire wing for her and her guards, but I have the feeling she's going to want to spend time with us."

"That's good."

"It is?" he asked.

"Out on Bella" —I sighed— "before everything happened, Josefina told me that her favorite job was being a mother." A smile came to my lips. "I don't think I realized until I learned my mom was out of prison, but I'd like a mom around. Since Josefina is available, it works out."

After depositing his array of weapons, Rei slipped out of his boots and dark jeans. Forgetting about my book, I scanned from his wide shoulders to his toned abs and all the way down to the noticeable bulge in his boxer briefs.

Tugging my lip between my teeth, I said what had been on my mind since before we arrived to the place we could call home. "I want you inside me."

Rei's eyes opened wide. "Well, *Señora* Roríguez, I appreciate your straightforwardness."

"It's just that you said it was up to me, and..."

The last few nights we've mostly held one another. There was kissing and petting, but also the sense that we needed to grieve. Jorge's birth brought spirit back to this family, the hope that life continued even in the darkest of times.

I was ready to move on if Rei was.

After stepping into the bathroom for a minute, Rei

was back, wearing only his boxer briefs. He didn't need to say he was ready. The way his dark gaze was set on me left my flesh covered in goose bumps. Beginning at the end of the king-sized bed, he crawled toward me. Hand, knee, hand, knee. His gaze never left mine. With each progression, my pulse increased.

Rei was a man deprived of the one thing we hadn't done, and I'd blurted out my permission. The fresh scent of soap and mint of toothpaste preceded his contact by a millisecond. Our lips crashed together, two people starved for what only the other could provide. His kiss sizzled and bruised my lips, stealing my breath. Noses bumped and our hands roamed until his settled in my long hair, twisting it and tugging my head back.

His lips came to my neck, igniting flames from the embers that had been lying dormant. Lying over me, his erection probed my stomach as he continued his torturous assault from my neck to my collarbone and lower. Pushing the straps of my nightgown away, his lips sought my breasts.

Electricity shot through me as he sucked one nipple and then the next. I wove my fingers through his mane as his facial hair abraded my sensitive skin and dampened my core.

Rei's approving hiss filled the room as his fingers rubbed over the crotch of my panties. "You're fucking soaked." He crawled lower, dragging the waistband of my panties down my legs. Sitting up on his heels, his tenor changed. "Spread your legs, *preciosa*. Let me see that virgin pussy." His lips curled. "It will never be virgin again."

His commanding tone had my circulation on fire. I spread my legs.

"Move your knees up."

He helped direct me until I was holding each knee.

"Your pussy is so wet, you're dripping." Without warning, he lowered his face.

I called out his name as he lapped my folds. Instinctively, I let go of my knees and tried to close my thighs, an impossible task with his wide shoulders blocking my movement. His actions were determined. Rei was a starving man, and I was his meal.

The pressure within me began to build. "Rei, I'm going to come." I reached for his head. "Please, I want you inside me."

All at once, his lips were on mine, sharing my own taste. I wasn't certain when he'd taken off his boxer briefs, but as his tongue sought entrance between my lips, the hardened rod of his penis pressed between my folds.

I gasped at the new pressure.

Rei lifted his body until our gazes met. "Breathe, Jasmine."

Biting my lip, I nodded.

"Look at me."

His intense dark stare became my focus.

"I meant what I said before. I want you to like this."

I gritted my teeth and arched my back as he pushed farther inside me.

I wasn't sure but maybe if he did it fast.

His fingers stroked my hair as he left butterfly kisses on my cheeks and neck. The pain subsided slowly as a different kind of sensation awakened. His continued motion caused friction rubbing over my clit, relighting the earlier fire and sending shock waves in every direction. There was a connection in what we were doing that eased the pain. Looking into his eyes, I smiled. "It's better."

I concentrated on his movements, the feeling of loss as he pulled partially away and the immense sense of fullness when he thrust within. His patience and ease worked as I began to move with his rhythm, pressing against him and backing away.

My hands roamed over the muscles of his back down to his tight ass. The noises and sounds were a chorus as the tension built.

Rei's movements became less fluid and more erratic. It was as he stilled that I looked up at his exquisite face twisted in pleasure that I knew this was something I would enjoy. His cock throbbed within me. Seeing the recent stress and sorrow melt away into a beautiful expression was more than enough to want to do this over and over.

His muscles relaxed as he rolled to my side, breaking our connection. Immediately, he was back to stroking my hair and staring into my eyes. "Tell me that you're okay."

I rolled to face him. "Better than okay."

When he started to move, I panicked. "Where are you going?"

"I'll be right back."

In the bathroom, I heard the water running. Rei returned in all his naked glory with a washcloth in hand. He moved the blankets. "Let me…"

The washcloth came into view, the white covered with a pink hue.

"I'm bleeding?"

"It's not bad." He lowered his face to mine. "You'll be sore" —his lips quirked— "but I'll be happy to kiss it all better."

After taking the washcloth back to the bathroom, Rei got under the covers and pulled me to his hard shoulder. "I don't know how I would have gotten through the last few weeks without you."

I lifted my face to his. "I love being here with you. But the world, it scares me."

Rei nodded. "I keep thinking about what would have happened if you, *Madre*, and Mia had been on Bella. Jorge saved your lives."

I sighed. "Maybe if we wouldn't have taken four of the guards with us, they could have fended off the Russians."

He squeezed me to his side and kissed the top of my head. "You don't remember what you asked me when you were roofied, do you?"

Pressing my lips together, I shook my head. "I don't remember any of it. It's like I went from sitting at the bar in the restaurant to waking in my bed. Everything in between is gone."

"You asked me if I could love you."

"Oh..." I buried my face against his side.

Rei reached for my chin. "I told you yes."

Tears prickled my eyes. "You said yes?"

"Then you told me that you could love me too." He inhaled. "The people who never knew him are saying so many awful things about *mí padre*, and yet that wasn't the person *mí madre* loved. I do bad things, Jasmine. I could understand if you didn't think you could love me."

Lifting myself up on my elbows, I stroked his cheek with my finger. "I could love you, Rei, and I already do. I was so afraid that something had happened to you. When you walked into Mia's hospital room, my world was complete. I love you."

He nodded. "I was afraid too. I'm not supposed to admit that, but I was. When we first heard about the distress call, all I could think about was that I took you to Bella to be safe and you weren't."

A memory of Dario telling me that men like him and possibly Rei could be both fearless and terrified came to mind. I laid my head back on Rei's shoulder. "Some of the strongest men I know can't admit to also being terrified or it takes them a long time. I think admitting emotions makes you even stronger."

"*Mí padre* used to say that loving someone creates a weakness in the armor." He inhaled. "It was what we did, knowingly attacking Herrera's family." Rei squeezed me tighter. "You're my weakness. I'd burn this world to ashes for you. I love you, Jasmine."

"I love you, too."

EPILOGUE

Reinaldo
Three months later

"I'm not going to lie, having you naked in my arms in your childhood bedroom with the capo in the next room is a bit...unnerving."

Jasmine wiggled under the blankets, her petite hand moving down my torso, finding my hard cock. As one hand moved up and down the shaft, she peppered my chest with kisses, her lips moving lower.

"You're trying to get me killed. Is that it?"

She shook her head, her flowing long red hair tickling my skin as her kisses went lower still. All at once I rolled us, me landing on top as I lowered myself, my mouth landing right at the height of her perky round breasts. She shrieked when I sucked one nipple. As it hardened and she squirmed, I took a playful nip.

Jasmine's laughter filled the room.

"I sure as fuck hope these walls are soundproof."

My wife cupped my cheeks. "I never heard Dario through the wall."

"Because he's an old man."

"We're here to celebrate Ariadna Gia's first birthday," she reminded me. "I'd say he can still get it up."

I sucked her other nipple, causing Jasmine to writhe. "He probably needs those pills they advertise on TikTok."

She scrunched her nose. "I don't want to think about that." Jasmine's finger came to my lips. "No more talking about anyone's sex life but ours." She fisted my cock. "You don't need pills."

"I do not."

She ran her hands over my arms and shoulders as I took my time, kneading her breasts and tweaking her nipples. It was as my hand found its way down to her silky, wet pussy that Jasmine gasped, her bright blue eyes intent on me.

I noticed the red patches on her porcelain flesh. "You're so fucking beautiful with your skin reddened by my beard."

Her lips curled. "I like the way your beard feels on my skin, especially in extra-sensitive areas."

"You want me to eat your pussy?"

Pink flowed from her neck to her cheeks as she nodded. "I like it when you do that. It helps me relax so I can handle your giant cock."

"I am giant, but you don't know that. You don't have any comparisons."

"I don't want any comparisons." Her expression turned sultry. "I want you."

"Oh, *preciosa*, you have me." I kissed down the valley between her tits, over the swell of each one, lower to the flat planes of her stomach, and made my way down to her sweet, wet pussy. Her hips bucked as I lapped her essence and twirled her clit with my tongue. It was when Jasmine's back arched and she clawed for the sheets that I moved my way over her and thrust deep inside her.

Jasmine reared up, hugging my neck as she stifled a scream on my shoulder. Her fingernails clung to my shoulders as I pistoned my hips, faster and faster. The friction of her tight cunt was on the edge of painful before morphing to ecstasy.

If she was trying to stay quiet, my wife was failing fantastically. I fucking loved the sounds she made when we were joined as one. There were high notes and bass notes. The moans and the whimpers. Each noise was the prelude and then the chorus. It was as the sounds grew higher and their speed of delivery increased that I knew my wife was almost there.

I watched her magical expression.

Her fingernails dug deeper into my skin seconds before her lips formed the perfect "o," and she shuddered around me. The sensation sent me over the edge, her pussy milking my cock as I filled her to overflowing. Muscle by muscle, Jasmine relaxed, her satiated smile shone up at me as her blue eyes swirled with sated dark blue circles. Despite us both being fulfilled, I lingered where I was, content with our union.

Teasing strands of her fiery red hair away from her

face, I found myself mesmerized by the woman I called my wife. "I think about how close I was to losing you."

She shook her head. "You didn't."

"I think that I love you with all my capability to love, and then the next day, the next smile" —I caressed her cheek— "the next time we're together like this, I realize it's more than I loved you yesterday. I don't know if it will ever stop being more."

"I hope not."

Wincing at the loss of connection, I pulled out and rolled to Jasmine's side.

"Have you decided if we're going to tell Dario and Cat?" I asked.

Jasmine buried her face in my shoulder. "Mia warned me." She lifted her face to mine. "Roríguez men are definitely fertile."

A scoff caused my chest to jiggle. "We can wait to let them know." I lowered my hand to her stomach. "You're not showing at all, except for your boobs. If anything, you seem skinnier."

"Contessa told me I need to eat."

"*Mí madre* won't tell."

Jasmine couldn't hide the pregnancy from *mí mamá*, as she suffered serious morning sickness in the beginning. As a matter of fact, *Madre* called the pregnancy before we did.

"I know, but since Josefina knows, I feel like Dario and Catalina should too."

"And then I can tell Jano and Mia." I smoothed Jasmine's silky hair. "Just think, our baby can grow up with Ariadna Gia and Jorge as cousins."

"This alliance certainly knows how to procreate."

As I was almost asleep, Jasmine asked, "Did you notice Isabella at dinner tonight?"

Isabella Luciano.

"Is this a trick question?"

She sat up, exposing her luscious growing breasts. "No, why would it be a trick question?"

"Because Dario wanted me to marry…" I pressed my lips together. "Never mind, I saw her but didn't particularly notice her."

Jasmine's eyebrows danced. "I think Em did. They were talking by the fireplace."

I let out a sigh. "Do you think Carmine will stand by his word and allow her to marry?"

"I've never liked Carmine or Salvatore, but the final word is Dario's."

"Hopefully, the capo's forgiven Em for taking you to the Green Lady Lounge."

Jasmine giggled. "He's forgiven you."

I ran my hand over her soft skin. "Do you think the capo will want to be called *abuelo*?" I lifted my brows. "Grandpa."

"I don't know."

I kissed her hair. "Good night, *Señora* Roríguez. I love you."

"Buenas noches, *mí marido*." She rubbed her nose against mine. "Did I say that right?"

"*Sí, mi esposa. Estarás hablando español cuando nuestro bebé se gradúe de la universidad.*"

"That was yes, right?"

My cheeks rose in a grin. "That was yes."

. . .

Thank you for reading QUEENS AND MONSTERS, Reinaldo and Jasmine's story and the ongoing saga of the Luciano famiglia and Roríguez cartel. Be sure to pre-order TO HAVE AND TO HOLD and learn if Emiliano will finally get his HEA as more dangerous trials test the alliance.

If you haven't read the earlier couples' stories, download NOW AND FOREVER, Dario and Catalina's story, TILL DEATH DO US PART, Aléjandro and Mia's story, and BOUND BY A PROMISE, Dante and Camila's story.

WHAT TO DO NOW

Visit Aleatha's store to purchase e-books, signed books, and store exclusive items. Link available on her website: aleatharomig.com

LEND IT: Did you enjoy *QUEENS AND MONSTERS*? Do you have a friend who'd enjoy *QUEENS AND MONSTERS*? *QUEENS AND MONSTERS* may be lent one time. Sharing is caring!

RECOMMEND IT: Do you have multiple friends who'd enjoy my dark romance with twists and turns and an all new sexy and infuriating anti-hero? Tell them about it! Call, text, post, tweet...your recommendation is the nicest gift you can give to an author!

REVIEW IT: Tell the world. Please go to the retailer where you purchased this book, as well as Goodreads, and write a review. Please share your thoughts about *QUEENS AND MONSTERS* on:

*Amazon, *QUEENS AND MONSTERS* Customer Reviews

*Barnes & Noble, *QUEENS AND MONSTERS,* Customer Reviews

*iBooks, *QUEENS AND MONSTERS* Customer Reviews

* BookBub, *QUEENS AND MONSTERS* Customer Reviews

*Goodreads.com/Aleatha Romig

Visit Aleatha's store to purchase e-books, signed books, and store exclusive items. Link available on her website: aleatharomig.com

BRUTAL VOWS:

NOW AND FOREVER

May 2024

TILL DEATH DO US PART

June 2024

BOUND BY A PROMISE

October 2024

QUEENS AND MONSTERS

January 2025

TO HAVE AND TO HOLD

March 2025

SINCLAIR DUET:

REMEMBERING PASSION

September 2023

REKINDLING DESIRE

October 2023

ROYAL REFLECTIONS SERIES:

RUTHLESS REIGN

November 2022

RESILIENT REIGN

January 2023

RAVISHING REIGN

April 2023

RELEVANT REIGN

June 2023

SIN SERIES:

RED SIN

October 2021

GREEN ENVY

January 2022

GOLD LUST

April 2022

BLACK KNIGHT

June 2022

STAND-ALONE ROMANTIC SUSPENSE:

LIGHT DARK

Republished 2024

Previously: INTO THE LIGHT and AWAY FROM THE DARK

SILVER LINING

October 2022

KINGDOM COME

November 2021

DEVIL'S SERIES (Duet):

DEVIL'S DEAL

May 2021

ANGEL'S PROMISE

June 2021

SPARROW WEBS

WEB OF SIN:

SECRETS

October 2018

LIES

December 2018

PROMISES

January 2019

TANGLED WEB:

TWISTED

May 2019

OBSESSED

July 2019

BOUND

August 2019

WEB OF DESIRE:

SPARK

Jan. 14, 2020

FLAME

February 25, 2020

ASHES

April 7, 2020

DANGEROUS WEB:

Prequel: "Danger's First Kiss"

DUSK

November 2020

DARK

January 2021

DAWN

February 2021

THE INFIDELITY SERIES:

BETRAYAL

Book #1

October 2015

CUNNING

Book #2

January 2016

DECEPTION

Book #3

May 2016

ENTRAPMENT

Book #4

September 2016

FIDELITY

Book #5

January 2017

THE CONSEQUENCES SERIES:

CONSEQUENCES

(Book #1)

August 2011

TRUTH

(Book #2)

October 2012

CONVICTED

(Book #3)

October 2013

REVEALED

(Book #4)

Previously titled: Behind His Eyes Convicted: The Missing Years

June 2014

BEYOND THE CONSEQUENCES

(Book #5)

January 2015

RIPPLES **(Consequences stand-alone)**

October 2017

CONSEQUENCES COMPANION READS:

BEHIND HIS EYES-CONSEQUENCES

January 2014

BEHIND HIS EYES-TRUTH

March 2014

~

STAND ALONE MAFIA THRILLER:

PRICE OF HONOR

Available Now

~

STAND-ALONE YA ROMANTIC THRILLER:

ON THE EDGE

May 2022

~

TALES FROM THE DARK SIDE SERIES:

INSIDIOUS

(All books in this series are stand-alone erotic thrillers)

Released October 2014

~

ALEATHA'S LIGHTER ONES:

PLUS ONE

Stand-alone fun, sexy romance

May 2017

ANOTHER ONE

Stand-alone fun, sexy romance

May 2018

ONE NIGHT

Stand-alone, sexy contemporary romance

September 2017

A SECRET ONE

Prequel to MY ALWAYS ONE

April 2018

MY ALWAYS ONE

Stand-Alone, sexy friends to lovers contemporary romance

July 2021

*QUINTESSENTIALLY THE ONE

Stand-alone, small-town, second-chance, secret baby contemporary romance

July 2022

*ONE KISS

Stand-alone, small-town, best friend's sister, grump/sunshine contemporary romance.

July 2023

*ONE STRING

Second-chance, enemies-to-lovers, fake-date, little-sister's-best-friend, forbidden, stand-alone contemporary romance

July 2024

ABOUT THE AUTHOR

Visit Aleatha's store to purchase e-books, signed books, and store exclusive items.

Aleatha Romig is a New York Times, Wall Street Journal, and USA Today bestselling author who lives in Indiana, USA. She has raised three children with her high school sweetheart and husband of over thirty years. Before she became a full-time author, she worked days as a dental hygienist and spent her nights writing. Now, when she's not imagining mind-blowing twists and turns, she likes to spend her time with her family and friends. Her other pastimes include reading and creating heroes/anti-heroes who haunt your dreams!

Aleatha impresses with her versatility in writing. She released her first novel, CONSEQUENCES, in August of 2011. CONSEQUENCES, a dark romance, became a best-selling series with five novels and two companions released from 2011 through 2015. The compelling and epic story of Anthony and Claire Rawlings has graced more than half a million e-readers. Her first stand-alone smart, sexy thriller INSIDIOUS was next. Then Aleatha released the five-novel INFIDELITY series, a romantic suspense saga, that took the reading world by storm, the final book landing on three of the top bestseller lists. She ventured into traditional publishing with Thomas and

Mercer. Her books INTO THE LIGHT and AWAY FROM THE DARK were published through this mystery/thriller publisher in 2016.

In the spring of 2017, Aleatha again ventured into a different genre with her first fun and sexy stand-alone romantic comedy with the USA Today bestseller PLUS ONE. She continued the "Ones" series with additional standalones, ONE NIGHT, ANOTHER ONE, MY ALWAYS ONE, QUINTESSENTIALLY THE ONE, ONE KISS, and ONE STRING.

If you like fun, sexy, novellas that make your heart pound, try her "Indulgence series" with UNCONVEN-TIONAL. UNEXPECTED, UNFORGETTABLE, and UNDENIABLE.

In 2018 Aleatha returned to her dark romance roots with SPARROW WEBS. And continued with the mafia romance DEVIL'S DUET, and most recently her Brutal Vows series.

You may find all Aleatha's titles on her website.

Aleatha is a "Published Author's Network" member of the Romance Writers of America and PEN America. She is represented by SBR Media and Dani Sanchez with Wildfire Marketing.

facebook.com/aleatharomig

instagram.com/aleatharomig